Sara G. Chafa

Napoleon Bonaparte

and other poems

Sara G. Chafa

Napoleon Bonaparte
and other poems

ISBN/EAN: 9783337349714

Printed in Europe, USA, Canada, Australia, Japan

Cover: Foto ©Andreas Hilbeck / pixelio.de

More available books at **www.hansebooks.com**

OTTO WAGNER, PHOTO.   NEW YORK.

Napoleon Bonaparte

AND OTHER POEMS.

BY

SARA GENEVRA CHAFA.

CAMBRIDGE:
PRINTED AT THE RIVERSIDE PRESS.
1872.

RIVERSIDE, CAMBRIDGE:
STEREOTYPED AND PRINTED BY
H. O. HOUGHTON AND COMPANY.

CONTENTS.

NAPOLEON BONAPARTE.

"Thou art Freedom's now, and Fame's,
One of the few, the immortal names
That were not born to die." — F. G. HALLECK.

CANTO THE FIRST.

ON an isle begirt by ocean,
Where the waves in restless motion
      Dash against the shore ;
When the people had uprisen,
And had sacked this spot Elysian,
And each dwelling was a prison,
      Or was dreaded more ;
'Mid these scenes of blood and sorrow,
Darker growing every morrow,
There was born a child whom Fate
Had ordained to high estate.
Though when first he breathed the air
'Round him shone the battle's glare,
And he heard such thrilling sound
As when swords from scabbards bound,
Born 'mid tumult, 'twas to be
Raised, afar from Corsica,
To a royal destiny.

I

Riot runs o'er sunny France,
And on graves the people dance;
Ne'er before saw Heaven a sight
Equal that in horror quite.
Men seemed demons, and each form
Helped to spread the awful storm;
Drunk with blood, they wildly cursed
Those who did not do their worst;
And poor France became a hell,
And the people graced it well.
Lo! they dare to mock at GOD,
For, above each grave-yard sod,
There are words of import deep:
"Death is an eternal sleep."

He who sat upon the throne,
Listening to his people's groan,
Durst not call his life his own,
    For the mass was maddened.
Scaffolds raised their gory heads,
Graves were then the softest beds
    Which the nobles gladdened.
Beauty, wealth, and lofty mien
Graced the horrid guillotine.
To this scene of wild confusion,
From a young life's strange seclusion,
    Came the hero of my song;
Came to this distracted land,
Guided by an Unseen Hand,
    To oppose the wrong.
Sunny France before him lay

Stained with blood by night and day,
And his eagle eye took in
All its misery, all its sin,
And with mighty grasp of mind
Revolutions he combined.
Gifts or gold he never sought,
With his own o'er-mastering thought
All his fame himself he wrought.

Riot rose around the wall
Of the nation's capitol,
And the king and nobles found
People will not all be bound,
And crushed in the trodden ground.
High as heaven there rose the shout,
" Lead the King and Nobles out ! "
" Blood ! " yes, " blood ! " they fiercely cried, —
And the King and Nobles died.

Lo ! through the streets of Paris came
A hissing thunder-burst of flame,
And pavement stones are covered o'er
With seething streams of human gore.
Guiding all this work of death
Stands Napoleon, with hushed breath,
Watching with a kindling eye
As the mob in terror fly ;
For that dreadful fire had mown
Heaps on heaps of wretches down,
Nothing mortal could oppose
Such unlooked for, awful blows.

France was now a heaving flood ;
Surge on surge broke seas of blood ;
Was there one with strength to guide
This terrific, human tide ?
Yes ! a man stepped from the crowd
(He to whom the mob had bowed),
And that fearful mass of life
Moved in order to the strife.
Europe trembles at the scene,
For her thrones o'er chasms lean ;
But the downtrod of all lands
Clinch their pained and shackled hands, —
And with anxious, prayerful eyes,
Lifted toward the darkened skies,
Wait the blow which can but be
Herald of their liberty.

As the conqueror's course grew bright,
Kings were seized with much affright ;
It were difficult to know
How to crush so strange a foe ;
One toward whom their subjects' eyes
Turned with longing and surprise,
And before whom enemies
Sank as swallowed by the seas.

Lofty were his plans to save
France from a dishonored grave,
And the people, crushed so long,
Raised a loud, rejoicing song ;
That one name, unknown before,

Roused the land from shore to shore.
" Savior ! Friend ! " they wildly cried ;
And the echo has ne'er died ;
Bonaparte is loved to-day
Almost with idolatry.

Soon in every home in France
Glad lips spoke of his advance ;
Yet united nations stood
Banded for his country's blood ;
    Ready with uplifted hand
To crush down " the people's friend,"
Fearing lest his fame extend,
    And he save his trembling land.

France was pierced on every side,
England mocked the people's pride,
Austria did her strength deride,
And, ere long, a blood-red tide
Lashed her shores both far and wide.
Yet amid this clash of arms,
    And the bugle's martial notes,
Lo ! love's voice, most soft and sweet,
    O'er Napoleon's spirit floats.
To the dream awhile he yields,
And forgets fierce battle-fields ;
Fairer spots he now doth tread,
    Softened tones beguile his ear,
Angels hover overhead, —
    At his side is one more dear.
'Tis the lovely Josephine

Who so glorifies the scene,
And whose constant tenderness
Shall his stormy future bless.
With her wifely words of pride
    Thrilling through his inmost soul,
Soon he hastes the tide to stem,
    Threatening over France to roll.
At her frontiers thousands stood
Eager for the nation's blood ;.
Bayonets flashed where foes without
Did to civil traitors shout ;
France indeed stood trembling o'er
    Horror, anarchy, and death ;
Cannon shook her rocky shore,
    Till the bravest held their breath.[1]
Yet Napoleon stood up, proud
That this darkly gathering cloud
Backward by his hand should roll ;

[1] "England with her invincible fleet was hovering around
the coast of the Republic, assailing every exposed point, land-
ing troops upon the French territory, and arming and inspiring
the Royalists to civil war. Austria had marched an army of.
nearly two hundred thousand men upon the banks of the Rhine,
to attack France on the north ; she had called into requisition
all her Italian possessions, and, in alliance with the British
navy, and the armies of the King of Sardinia, and the fanatic
legions of Naples and Sicily, had gathered eighty thousand men
upon the Alpine frontier. It was purely a war of self-defense
on the part of the French people. They were contending
against the bullets and bayonets of the armies of monarchical
Europe assailing them at every point. Napoleon had but
thirty thousand men to repel these eighty thousand invaders."
—J. S. C. ABBOTT.

And his clear, far-reaching soul
Felt, in all this clash of war,
What *he* had uprisen for.
Did he, as historians tell,
Seek to make a very hell
Of the earth whereon he trod,
And poor France, which mocked at God?
No! he sought, did all but pray,
This red tide of war to stay.
But the young Republic shook
　With the gathering despots' tread,
And the French, with dauntless look,
　Placed Napoleon at their head,
And with bosoms beating high
　With a superhuman love,
Vowed for France to stand and die,
　While one eagle perched above
One stout form, with strength to ride
By their chosen chieftain's side.
Cottage hearth, and palace hall
Quickly answered Freedom's call;
From each home a warrior sprung,
　And with hurrying steps sped on
To the sound of rolling drum —
　Sped from faces pale and wan;
Tearful maidens, white-browed wives,
Gave France thirty thousand lives;
Gave them with a lofty pride,
Sent them bravely from each side;
Every eye gleamed with fierce fire,
　Every foot with gladness sped,

Every brow grew dark with ire
When their chief, whom they adored,
Pointed to the gathering horde,
And in words like sword-thrusts, said,
"We must fight, or France is dead!"

SONG OF THE FRENCH SOLDIERS.

Brothers! Frenchmen! haste to battle,
  For the foe has reached the border;
Yonder rides our gallant chieftain,
  Marshaling the ranks in order.
Signal fires burn on the hill-tops,
  Squadrons tramp adown the valley;
Forward, Frenchmen! arm, and forward!
  'Tis Napoleon bids you rally.

England's fleets distress our harbors,
  Northern Europe comes to greet her;
Where 's the foe a Frenchman feareth?
  Injured Frenchmen! rise to meet her!
Honor to "the little Corporal!"
  Where he leads what heart will falter?
Vive la France! march forward, comrades!
  And we'll die upon her altar.

Loyally did France uprise
To repel her enemies;
Rose and followed this one man,

Whose career had just began.
Swords and battlements seemed rife
With a living, moving life ;
E'en the cannon seemed to say,
France ne'er yields to despot sway.
Horse and foot, a flying mass,
Onward toward the frontiers pass.

Naught could stand before his wrath,
Blood and conquest marked his path,
And unto the conqueror proud
Austria's Emperor humbly bowed.
For his army swiftly fell,
Danger hemmed the capitol,
Bands of the victorious foe
Thirsted for his overthrow,
And to save poor Austria
From a further sacrifice,
He must now accept of peace
From a foe he dared despise.

France was victor ! joy-bells rung,
And one name was on each tongue.
Widows, blind with scalding tears,
Listened to the crashing cheers,
And then turned with mournful pride
To the rocking cradle's side.
Maidens decked their brows of snow
With the cypress wreath of woe,
Then turned with a flush of pride to see
The returning " Army of Italy."

Yet within the nation's halls,
  There were some, historians tell us,
Who denounced Napoleon's fame,
  Of "the little Corporal" jealous ;[1]
And, when peace had come to bless
France with wealth and happiness,
They did proffer and portray,
Grander conquests far away.
"Seek you Egypt's shores," said they,
"And establish in the land
Empires worthy of command.
Oriental legions wait
For the favored one of Fate.
Hasten there, and there extend
Thy glory as ' the people's friend.'
Success magnificent shall be
Thy country's, thine, across the sea."

Soon the soldiers, tried and true,
With Napoleon bade adieu
To the shores of bonny France,
With a longing, onward glance.
Peals of acclamations rung
While the fleet in moorings swung ;
And when over ocean blue
Sail nor mast doth meet the view,

---

[1] " The Directory were made exceedingly uneasy by ominous expressions in the streets, ' We will drive away these lawyers and make the *little Corporal* king.' These cries wonderfully accelerated the zeal of the Directory in sending Napoleon to Egypt ; and most devoutly did they hope that from that distant land he would never return." — J. S. C. ABBOTT.

Countless bosoms, as one heart,
Beat with love for Bonaparte.

Now among the nations France
Stood as one awoke from trance;
Industry began to stir,
And a ceaseless buzz and whirr,
Told that peaceful life again
Once more filled the smiling plain.

. . . .

Over ocean's heaving tide
Gallantly those good ships ride,
Bearing to Egyptian sands
Bold, adventurous, eager bands,—
Bands who followed, loved, and wrought
For this man of giant thought.
Egypt's shores at length are seen
Waves and firmament between;
For beneath the blazing sun
Waves and sky appear as one.
Naught but bleak and burning sands
Greets the army as it lands,
Save when scattering Arabs scour
O'er the desert at 'mid hour,
And with strange, unearthly cry,
Wheel beneath the burning sky,
As before the startled eye
Bayonets flash, and banners fly.
Music grand and martial song,
O'er the desert roll along,

And the well-trained soldiers move
'Neath the eye of him they love.

In a lone Egyptian bay
Quietly the French fleet lay,
Manned with spirits, firm and brave,
Proud to fill a soldier's grave,
While their dauntless comrades face
Danger in the desert place.

England, with a jealous eye,
   Watched the rising star of France,
And with dread, lest light should spread,
   Scanned with fear this bold advance.
Soon her ships, unnumbered, ride
On the great sea's swelling tide,
Seeking for the fleet which lay
Moored within that Eastern bay.
All unknowing of the storm
French battalions march and form ;
Over deserts parched with heat
Tread the weary soldiers' feet,
While beside, with sweatless brow,
   Watching them with loving eye,
Toils Napoleon through the sand,
   Blessed by those who, falling, die.
Many a corpse with ghastly look
Marked the course the army took,
For the simoon's burning breath
Swiftly did the work of death ;

Waves and winds, and sun and thirst,
Seemed as bent to do their worst;
But despite them all, at last,
Is the parching desert passed,
And beneath the brazen sky
Form the French triumphantly.

BATTLE OF THE PYRAMIDS.

The granite obelisks looked down one day
  Upon a sight to be remembered yet, —
The marshaling for a terrible affray,
  Where two strong hosts in mortal combat met.
The sunlight glared upon the burning sand,
  Upon unnumbered warriors, fierce and proud,
On jet black steeds, and on a silent band
  Who waited sternly for the battle cloud.

Strong, dense, and furious was the pagan host;
  Armed, mounted, dark, a fearful sight to see;
A common foe could only hope, at most,
  For graves, for few had thought of victory.
In solid squares the French troops quickly form;
  They never were defeated, nor must be;
Napoleon is their god: he fears no storm,
  And this his motto, *Die, but never flee!*

Their squares are firm, their bristling bayonets
    bright,
And thus they wait those ranks of cavalry

Which, moving now, a most terrific sight,
Sweep o'er the sand with awful majesty.
Napoleon shouts, " Remember, men, to-day,
That ages from those Pyramids look down ! "
That was enough, and naught of earth could stay
The tide which crowned their arms with grand
renown.

The Turks came on to meet a wall of steel,
And squares unshaken as an ocean rock ;
They plunge, they rear, some fall ; at last they
reel
And stagger back before the mighty shock.
Again they charge ; again the fearless foe
Hurl back the bleeding mass that yet remain, —
Along the sand the dead are lying low,
And under foot the wounded shriek with pain.

But useless all ; like ocean's dashing waves
Those horsemen plunge, and reel, and plunge
again ;
They only gain, spite all their efforts, graves,
And blood which flows like equinoctial rain.
O, valiant French ! the ages well may tell
Thy deeds, where Pyramids were looking down ;
Ye fought so bravely, and so bravely fell, —
Historic pens must e'er accord renown.

The pagan host, which proudly sought the fray,
Is crushed and scattered, broken, bleeding, lost ;
The French have won, have glorified the day ;
And yet, alas ! at what a fearful cost.

They naught withheld, and naught did grudge to
    give,
  To prove their faith in him, their chosen Chief: —
The Battle of the Pyramids will live
  So long as winds shall wave one laurel leaf.

    .   .   .   .

   In the Pasha's royal hall
    Sat a man of iron thought,
  And for Superstition's fall
    Planned and wrought, planned and wrought,
      With his concentrated might
      Crushing wrong, upraising right,
      Till the rude Arab and Turk
      Gladly bowed before his work,
      And Napoleon's dreaded name
      Soon a sound of love became.
      Not a spoiler's hand was felt
      Where a heathen goddess knelt ;
      Roving Mameluke was still
      Free to worship at his will,
      And the prosperous country lay
      Smiling 'neath Napoleon's sway,
      While poor France grew weak again
      For the want of this one man.

      Anchored in a sunny bay,
      On one memorable day,   .
      Rode the fleet which bore the man
      All the nations turned to scan.
      Brave old tars, with hearts of will,
      Every vessel man and fill ;

But a proud, determined foe
Soon will sink them all below ;
Nelson, lord upon the sea,
Has decreed that this shall be.

BATTLE OF THE NILE.

Down o'er the waste of waters,
  Night settled dun and drear,
And the booming of the cannon
  Told the British fleet was near.

Each Frenchman knew what danger,
  And what awful tides of woe
Then threatened every vessel
  With the sea-weed shrouds below.

But not one firm lip quivered,
  Nor flashed one eye less bright ;
They had faced grim Death too often,
  And were eager for the fight.

The foe are stanch and ready,
  And with hot and lurid breath,
They form, and hasten forward
  To the Carnival of Death.

Lo, a flash ! A sound terrific
  O'er the gloomy water glides,
And answering flames burst swiftly
  From the French fleet's reeling sides.

The air is filled with thunder,
  With blood the water red,
There are gunners powder-blackened,
  There are piles of blackened dead.

There 's a glorious old Admiral,
  On the *Orient's* burning deck,
And with blood and flame surrounded
  He is gazing o'er the wreck.
'Till lo! a crash terrific,
  Like Heaven's grand reveille, —
Commander, crew, ships, vanish, —
  And "Britannia rules the sea."

Evil news will travel fast,
  And when this Napoleon heard,
How the battle had been lost,
  Scarcely uttered he a word.
Just a moment o'er his face
There were signs of anxiousness;
Just a moment; then the shock
Passed away, and like a rock
Stood the hero, calm and true,
Quick to plan, and strong to do.
   .   .   .   .

Form and forward! over the land
Rapidly spreads that brief command;
And eager bands march on and form
To breast the gathering eastern storm;

2

From serried ranks, from compact square,
Bright blades flash in the heated air;
And with devotion such as ne'er
Before 'shrined monarch, priest, or seer,
They gather round, a mass of life,
Their chief to follow to the strife.
Ah! woe to foe and joy to friend,
For those proud ranks nor shake nor bend;
And backward reeled Arab and Turk
Before Napoleon's giant work.
The nations wondered; England ground
Her teeth in rage, and at one bound
Jumped "constitution" in advance,
And swore eternal hate to France.

Then it was the northern sky
　Glowed again with war's red flame,
And grim Revolution cried,
　Cried aloud Napoleon's name.
O'er the land it seemed to roll,
Thrilling each heroic soul,
Bowing those who sat in state
Like a thunderbolt of fate.
Nothing now that cry could still,
Which, from valley, plain, and hill,
　Rose and crossed the sea;
This the burden of the call
Which shook Senate-house and Hall:
"Where, O, where is he,
Egypt's Savior, despot's fear,
　Truest friend of Italy?"

"France convulsed? I cannot stay!
Farewell Egypt! I'll away!
Soldiers, rally! o'er the sea
There is need of you and me.
Haste! your Chief ne'er led to shame —
Barbarous Egypt now is tame."
Such his words ; let no man say
That "the coward ran away ; "
As historians have belied
Him whose strongest trait was pride,
Joined with courage, which could dare
Danger any, everywhere ;
For his cautious moves, condemned
By his critics, foe and friend,
Only led him safely through
Those in wait on ocean blue.

Often in this journey home,
When the ocean's waves of foam
Rose' beneath the moon's pale light,
Did he, through the silent night,
Pace the deck with restless feet,
And to listening men repeat
Startling words of holy truth,
Fresh as when, in early youth,
He had listened with a thrill,
While, o'er native plain and hill,
Sweetest chime of Sabbath bell
On the still air rose and fell.
Like to one inspired did he
Point to starry canopy,

And, from all those brilliant spheres,
Rolling through the fleeting years,
Gather proof that hands divine
Led him 'long the shore of Time.

.   .   .   .

Hail, bonny France ! the danger 's past ;
Greet Napoleon, back at last !
Not a sail disturbed his sight
Of all Britain's boasted might ;
Softly lulled to passion's measure,
In the lap of amorous pleasure
Lay Lord Nelson, while the fleet
Of the French passed his retreat.

Storms without and storms within,
Now kept France in ceaseless din ;
But Napoleon grasped the helm,
    Wheeling round the Ship of State,
And the waves which would o'erwhelm
    Flowed from majesty so great.   .
Hostile armies formed outside,
Treason muttered far and wide,
Bonfires blazed upon the air,
And the Lion left his lair.
Europe stood, from bayonet-bands
Forging chains for Freedom's hands.
Lo ! her champion grandly rose
To disband these swarms of foes,
While his people, strong in right,
Fearing not the despots' might,

Crowd about his bold advance
Proclaiming him Consul of France.

Glory crowned, the land approved ;
But from her he fondly loved
   No glad messages were sent ;
Evil tongues, with venomed dart,
Kept these loving hearts apart,
   Clouding life's fair firmament.
She who bore, with wifely pride,
   Absence, ill, yea, anything,
That the world need not deride
   Its brave warrior, her heart's king,
Heard the cheers, the joyousness,
And bestowed not one caress.
But vile slander cannot part
Long, the constant, pure in heart.
Soon Napoleon clasps again
Her who soothes his fiercest pain,
Brightening e'en the darkest scene, —
Sorrowing, faithful Josephine.
" Rest, beloved ! " he murmurs low,
" Rest, sweet wife ! and ere I go
Forth to battle with the foe,
And to be where blood shall flow,
Hear me say, with Heaven above,
That 'tis thee alone I love."

CANTO THE SECOND.

THE battle 's fought; Marengo 's won;
And many an eye turns toward the sun
Veiled by the filmy hand of Death; ·
And many a fast departing breath
Disturbs the soul with sounds of woe,
Which only war-sacked plains can know.
The tide of blood had rolled that day
In waves it seemed no power could stay;
But everywhere one gleaming eye
Had guided war's wild revelry;
Had marked the closing columns' crash,
The wheeling squads, the cannon's flash,
The swaying flags, the failing foe,
The heaven above, the earth below.
And everywhere Death rode the gale,
And winds prolonged the dying's wail,
One face outshone serenely pale;
One steady voice cheered on the fight,
And nerved each arm with double might,
'Till soon, from out the sulphury night,
    Loud rang the cry of Victory!
Above the din, above the cloud,
It rolled in echoes long and loud,
And those wrapped in a bloody shroud
    Turned the fast glazing eye

To bless their Chieftain, home, and France,
Then sink in death's eternal trance.

.   .   .   .

Hasten! ye retreating foe!
Forward, French! to Linden's snow!
And the tide of war rolled on,
Rolled till peace at last was won.
Haughty Austria! humbled now,
To an uncrowned head, lo! bow;
Sign in truce thy royal name,
Take thy heritage of shame,
And thy fields of dead,
And thy homes whence joy has sped;
But reproach thine own ambition
For thine altered, sad condition;
Napoleon only fought that he
Might win for France equality.

Now, with one majestic stride,
    Back the mighty conqueror turns;
Moving down the Alps' rough side
    Still for Fame his bosom burns.
But not fame from bloody War
Is his soul outreaching for.
Monuments he planned to build
To the memory of the " Killed ";
Schools and churches he would found,
Bridges should unite the ground,
Mighty towers should grandly rise,
Stretching toward the sunny skies;
And sweet Peace (too soon it flies)
Should make France a Paradise.

Such *his* purpose ; but stern *fate*
Purposed more to make him great ;
Great with deeds less mild than these,
Great through blood like heaving seas,
Rolling o'er his own fair land,
Parted by his stern command,
That his hosts might walk the bed
Where its billows had been spread,
While his foes, engulfed from view,
Fain had had him o'erwhelmed too.
But some strange, some mighty power,
Which was manifest each hour,
Marked his path, with magic hand,
Full of thrones and sceptres grand ;
Yet it led through flame and smoke,
Cannon-flash, and sabre-stroke,
Things infernal and unseen,[1]
Fields of blood, such as, I ween,
Ne'er delighted Satan more,
· Or left man unscathed before.
What avail that peace was won ?
That the faces of the dead
On the trampled ground outspread,
And the hands whose work was done,
Ne'er reproached Napoleon ?
He had ‾sued of Europe's kings

---

[1] About this time was constructed the machine, called Infernal, which was intended to be exploded one night while Napoleon passed through the streets on his way to the theatre. It *did* explode, killing many and doing much other damage, but fortunately the Emperor escaped unhurt.

To be spared from such dread things.[1]
"Ah, he is afraid !" they said ;
Better they had all been dead,
Ere his leaden answer sped
Over Alps and Alpine snow,
To the peaceful plains below.

Words like these, words couched in blows,
Had at last brought France repose.
Such repose as cities feel
   Built upon volcanoes' breasts,
Ere the earthquake makes them reel
   At old Nature's high behests.
France had grown a mighty name,
Not a spot dimmed her fair fame ;
Pleasure smiled where war had raged,
Peace the people all engaged ;

[1] "When appointed First Consul by the French people he immediately wrote to the King of England, as follows : —

"' Called, Sire, by the wishes of the French nation, to occupy the first magistracy of the Republic, I judge it well on entering my office to address myself directly to your majesty. Must this war, which, for the last four years, has devastated the world, be eternal ? Are there no means of coming to an understanding ? How can the two most enlightened nations of Europe, stronger already, and more powerful than their safety or independence requires, sacrifice to ideas of vainglory the well being of commerce, internal prosperity, and the repose of families ? Your majesty will perceive only in this overture the sincerity of my desire to contribute efficaciously, for a second time, to the general pacification by this prompt advance.' To this magnanimous application for peace, the King of England did not judge it proper to return any personal answer. Lord Grenville replied in a letter full of the most bitter recriminations." — J. S. C. ABBOTT.

At each hearth one name alone
Oft was heard with " King " and " throne ; "
" Hail the people's truest friend ! "
" May his glory never end ! "
This the millions, all as one,
Shouted for Napoleon.

Too sweet was peace to triumph long ;
Down, down with Right ! up, up with Wrong !
Old Britain frowns ; 'tis not propïtious ;
" Napoleon 's getting too ambitious."
Send round again the bended bow,[1]
And drench again the land with woe.
War ! war ! yes, war to the death !
Spare not treasure, spare not breath.
Then it was that France uprose
In the face of swarming foes,
And, 'mid the gloom of Europe's frown,
Above the laurel placed a crown.
Then rose to heaven a mighty shout
While yet the thunder rolled about
The Empire's borders ; then began
Around their Chief to close each man,
And, desperate with love and pride,
Beat back the inward rolling tide.
Hark ! the deep-mouthed cannon's roar,
Wakes the echoing Alps once more ;

---

[1] It is supposed that war was anciently proclaimed in Britain by sending messengers in different directions, through the land, each bearing a bended bow. See the *Cambrian Antiquities.*

Valleys glow with bayonets' light,
Strong arms nerve them for the fight,
Fair hands wave a last good-by,
Pale lips hush the bitter cry
Of the tortured heart when giving
All for which that one is living.

'Mid an Empire's brilliant glare
Josephine grew pale with .care —
Thrones and crowns must have an heir.
Yet with soothing words sincere
Dries her lord each falling tear,
Calming every painful fear.
Then, as with a whirlwind's might,
Forth he goes to head the fight ; —
Palaces have sorrowing breasts,
Hearts are soft 'neath mailed vests ;
Deep his love for Josephine,
Deeper still for France, I ween.

England, on her island throne,
Heedless of the people's moan,
Proffered gold, and skill, and men,[1]
France to fill with war again.
Fiercely then Mars stamped his foot
Till the very Continent shook,
And all Europe now combined
To resist the march of mind.

---

[1] " All the wars of the European Continent against the Empire were begun by England, and supported by English gold." — *Encyclopædia Americana.*

From the North barbarian hordes
Joined with Austria's glittering swords ;
Prussian legions swarmed to fill
The Allied Army — band of ill-
United despots, boasting ever,
Deemed Napoleon lost forever.
Not so he ; with awful might,
Pausing not for day or night,
On he swept, invincible,
Toward Vienna's frowning wall.
Lo ! proud Austria's monarch fled ;
Onward still the victor sped,
'Till the world, with mouth agape,
Knew not where to mark the map.

AUSTERLITZ.

Dark and drear the night closed in ;
From the earth rose ceaseless din ;
An hundred thousand haughty foes
Have camped among those northern snows.
Lo ! what means that sudden light,
Gleaming through the gloomy night ;
Lighting far and wide the sky
With an untold brilliancy ? [1]

[1] "As Napoleon rode along the lines in the gloom of midnight, a soldier attached to his bayonet a bundle of straw, and
setting it on fire, raised the brilliant torch in the air. Instantly
the whole camp, extending for miles, blazed with illuminations,

Seventy thousand torches glare
In the creaking, wintry air;
Seventy thousand voices shout
" Vive l'Empereur ! " and about
Echo rolls the thrilling cry
Like a voice of prophecy.
  Night passed on ; morning broke,
Ushering in a day of wonder,
    Pointing through the fog and smoke
    To his men Napoleon spoke :
" We'll finish with a clap of thunder ! "
Soldiers, on ! the foemen reel
Before your gleaming lines of steel ;
Thus, confident of power and right,
Those legions headlong seek the fight.
They look to where their Emperor sits,
They shout, " The Sun of Austerlitz ! "
Then on — for, though his comrade fell,
Each felt himself invincible.
The foe is cut ; he breaks, he flies
Beneath the watching Emperors' eyes.
Some sink beneath an icy flood
    In fleeing from the field ;
Some lie in winding sheets of blood,
    And some as prisoners yield ;

as the soldiers elevated, flaming into the air, the straw provided
for their bivouacs. Transported with the enthusiasm of the
moment, the army raised a simultaneous shout, which, like
the roar of many waters, pierced the air, and vibrated in ominous thunders through the tents of the Allies." — J. S. C. AB-
BOTT.

And thus Napoleon in an hour
Destroys the Allied Army's power.
Peace was promised France once more ;
But Napoleon, who forebore
    To avail himself of might,
And extend his sceptre o'er
    Where his conquest gave him right,
Soon had reason to regret
    Acts of such compassion.[1]
Kings their treaties oft forget,
    Justified by fashion.
Though an empire had begun,
France was yet republican.
    And that she should dare to choose
For herself a low plebeian,
    And with bayonets refuse
To accept a Bourbon king !
That was cause enough to bring
Combined Europe's despots forth
From the great sea to the north.
Russia, Prussia, England then
Banded for the fight again.
Alex., from his borders wide,
Gathered up, with Czar-like pride,
Hordes of serfs, for centuries trod
Mindless, speechless, to the sod,
Which with Prussia's sons unite
In the coming, causeless fight.

---

[1] "In his vast conquests he had shown the most singular moderation, — a moderation which ought to have put England, Russia, and Prussia to the blush." — J. S. C. ABBOTT.

Reader, are you tired of blood
Flowing like a ceaseless flood?
So Napoleon was, though he
Fought almost continually,
And some oftentimes do say
He *loved* war — yet wherefore, pray?
Was't for fame? that would increase
From his works for France, *in peace.*
Was't for wealth? he needed none.
What then led Napoleon
To the battle-field again?
To Jena's trampled, bloody plain?
The haughty edict of his foes,
  · The right his crown to save,
His country's glory and repose,
    His subjects' honored graves.
Tired of war? Yet rouse thee, France!
Check thy foes, who fast advance!
On! Napoleon guides you yet. .
On! Hope's star has not yet set.
Form and forward! every man!
And again the red blood ran.
Bayonets bristled, cannon spoke
Through the sulphury clouds of smoke;
Loving eyes grew dim in death,
Heroes flung away their breath;
Cannon shook the hills around,
Bullets ploughed deep in the ground,
Frantic steeds, with furious neigh,
Galloped o'er where dead men lay;

Batteries belched, and columns broke,
Banners flaunted in the smoke,
Death-cries mingled with the crash
Of the charging squadron's dash.
Everywhere, with savage leer,
Death looks on the warrior's bier.
On Landgrafenberg's far height
Napoleon stands and rules the fight;
Guiding with his mighty mind
That vast sea of mad mankind.
Silent, stern, conscious of right,
He wields his awful arm of might ;
Russian and Prussian melt before
That arm, and sink to rise no more.
Night comes — the allied foe have fled ;
The few who sleep not with the dead,
Or, prisoners to the victor, wait
The captured soldier's weary fate.
The stars come out, the deed is done,
And France is saved, for Jena 's won.

.   .   .   .

Again Napoleon sues for peace ;
Again he gladly seeks release
From war, its agony intense
Of famine and of pestilence.
But the Czar's domains are wide,
Great his army, great his pride ;
And the Prussian Queen has power,
Wit and beauty for her dower :
Fill the broken ranks again,
And the plains with dying men.

Stopping just to pen a line
To the anxious Josephine,
In a few brief words to say
He had won a victory,
And he loved her tenderly ;[1]
Then dispelling every thought
Save those which were richly fraught
With the future weal of France,
To his troops he speaks, "Advance ! "
And resistlessly they pour
'Long Vistula's frozen shore.
Hostile batteries may oppose,
Countless miles of drifted snows,
Sheltered bands of deadly foes,
But their Chieftain's wondrous will
Makes each man invincible ;
Every heart is nerved by his
To accomplish prodigies.
What though marching to their graves !
Better this than live as slaves !
Eylau's horrors might appall
  Hearts of less devotion ;
But, though every soldier fall
  In the wild commotion,

---

[1] "Mon Amie, — Il y a eu hier une grande bataille ; la victoire m'est, mais j'ai perdu bien du monde ; la perte de l'ennemi qui est plus considérable · encore, ne me console pas. Enfin je t'écris ces 2 lignes moi-même, quoique je sois bien fatigué, pour te dire que je suis bien portant, et que je t'amie.
  "Tout a toi,   Napoleon.
"3 heures du matin le 9 Février."

3

None e'er grudged his life to give,
That, through him, his country live.

Words are weak the scene to paint ;
Gazing on it one grows faint ;
Gathered in the gloomy night,
Marshaling for the awful fight,
Covered o'er with whirling snow
Drifting on the sheets below,
Guided by the watchfires' light,
Legions seek the place assigned
By the ruling master-mind.
Morning shivers through the clouds
Hanging from the sky like shrouds ;
But the light that dimly broke
Soon was quenched in seas of smoke ;
Nature veiled her pallid face
O'er the scene by man defaced.
Still they battled ; still the tide
Ebbed and flowed on either side ;
Battled till the weary sun
    Sank in fright away,
Glad his sickening course was run,
    Glad to hide the day
From a world so black with crime
It did terrify old Time.

Why shock the reader more to tell ?
How many fought, how many fell ?
How the proud Allies, forced to flee,
Conceded France the victory ;

How she pursued with flame and smoke,
And this sixth coalition broke?
How Friedland lay a ruined heap,
And thousands slept a "dreamless sleep"
Amid the ice, among the snows,
Where Niemen river seaward flows?
How Alexander yielded then
To the most mighty of all men,
And, conquered both by arms and mind,
The Peace of Tilsit gladly signed.

. . . .

Brilliant grew the Empire's fame;
Brightly shone Napoleon's name;
On him gazed a world with awe
As he made for nations law;
People of less favored lands
Looked on his devoted bands
Through their tears, and longed to be
Where *worth* led to royalty.
Spain, long cursed with Bourbon sway,
Threw her jeweled crown away;
And her subjects, faction-rent,
Eyed fair France with discontent.
Well Napoleon knew that he
Must prepare for treachery,
And he wisely caught the crown
Which the Spanish Prince flung down.
Then the despots, all dismayed,
Whet again the battle blade.
England, ever in the van,
Places France beneath a ban,

And with all her fighting men
Soon prepares for war again.
Thus the crash of armies came
Shaking poor, voluptuous Spain,
Where unnumbered heroes fell
With nor sigh, nor sob, nor knell.
England made her lines of swords,
Prussia sent abroad her hordes,
Serf with despot did unite
Battling to oppose the right.
Thus they fought, determined all
That Napoleon's power should fall.
But, though England ruled the sea,
France did hold the victory
On the land, and showed her might
In each hurried, awful fight.
Still the loss of life, *so* great,
Made Napoleon curse his fate ;
And, so fast there gathered foes,
In his breast the thought arose,
Might he not restrain the tide
Rolling redly far and wide,
If to royal blood allied ?
Much he dreaded to remove
Her whom he so fondly loved,
And so long as hope remained
That by war peace might be gained,
He would meet his countless foes
With the weapons which they chose.
Was he not the people's choice ?
Did not nations then rejoice

'Neath his sway? and should he be
Forced to war eternally?

Traitors soon began to stir,
And a ceaseless clang and whirr
Rose aloft at Mars' dread call, —
France seemed one vast arsenal.
Back from Spain this mighty man
Hurriedly had come to scan,
And to crush (tremendous mission!)
A seventh great coalition.
Heaven again reflected light
From the bayonets, glistening bright;
Foundries burned far in the night,
Thousands armed them for the fight;
Armed and marched to meet a foe,
Which would lay an Empire low,
          And erect again
Bourbon thrones, with Bourbon kings, —
All those hateful, dreaded things,
          Over heaps of slain.

Some have called my countrymen
Heroes; tell me when, O when
Did Columbia's sons arise
Glorying in such sacrifice?
Battling long and patiently
Merely for equality?

          .   .   .   .

Once again the cannon's flash
Gleamed above the squadrons' dash;

Once again the batt'ries swept
  Ranks on ranks of heroes down ;
While the widow's children wept
  Tears to ornament a crown ;
And the "volleying thunder" spoke
Through the surging seas of smoke,
As if there it did invoke
Great Jehovah's curse on men,
Who could thus his laws condemn.

BATTLE OF ECKMUHL.

The sky is fair, the sun is rising bright,
  Dispelling silently a silver mist,
Which in the soft and stilly hours of night,
  Has sought the earth to wait his burning kiss.
  No penciled scene could fairer be than this, —
The blue above, the verdant earth below,
  As heaven and earth were keeping loving tryst ;
Alas ! they never weep o'er human woe,
Or grieve for that which men on fellow-man be-
    stow.

Could one have placed himself aloft that day,
  Far higher than the eagle's flight can be,
And had his power of sight been keen alway
  To pierce that rolling, rising, smoky sea,
  Though doubting God, he would have bent the
    knee,

And asked for might, or asked that He would
    veil
A scene so fraught with woe, it should but be
    Some old imaginary song, or tale,
Told with a stifled laugh to make young cheeks
    grow pale.

On spot so fair the battle-cloud had burst,
    Disclosing all its awfulness to view :
Fierce squadrons galloped o'er the plain where
    erst
    The timid birdlings unmolested flew.
The sun's warm rays, at noontide, drank the
    dew,
    When rolled the first deep cannon-tone ; and
    then
A livid burst of war came on and grew,
    'Till balls ploughed through such solid ranks
    of men,
One might have thought Jehovah justly slew,
Regardless, in his wrath, of e'en his chosen few.

The hills were shaken with the cannon's roar,
    And tramp of squadrons reeling to and fro ;
The ground grew red, and glared with human
    gore,
    And men forgot they were not down below,
Nor cared for shrieking friend, but sought the
    foe
    Through seas of smoke, and jets of falling
    flame ;

Wild grew each eye, and glad to watch the flow
  Of blood, and, shouting in the din Napoleon's
  name,
On rushed the French, and on the haughty Allies
  came.

They met; and earth, as with an earthquake's
    shock,
  Trembled beneath the crash which shook
    again
The hills, as though they were a wave-worn
  rock,
  Just toppling for a tumble in the main.
And shout, and curse, and shriek of awful pain,
  Rose o'er the thousand heavier sounds, as
    they,
Who yet are left to ride above the slain,
  Form, charge, and still with reckless fury slay,
And balance well the battle till the close of day.

Napoleon watches, plans, and guides each
    stroke ;
  He turns a look on his Imperial Guard,
Impatient gazing on each surge of smoke,
  With eyes of fire, and features stern and hard,
Clinched hands, set teeth, and many a visage
    scarred,
  With battle-scars.   He feels the moment 's
    near, —
" Charge ! Forward ! · On ! "   The Old Imperial
  Guard,

Dark, stately, massy, move without a cheer
Adown the sloping plain, and sweeping on, they
   near

And trample o'er their fallen comrades. See!
  From out the Allies' lines, a mass, as dark,
Comes forth like refluent billow of the sea
  And surges on sublimely grand ; and hark !
Hushed is each sound save those which mark
  The awful thrill each army feels. Each eye
Is riveted ; and dead men, stiff and stark,
  Might 'wake to look on such sublimity, —
For on those moving hosts Old Europe casts the
   die.

They meet, and clash! those living waves of
   men !
With foam of blood, and fiery flash of steel,
And smoke, which, as a shroud, envelops them
  From roaring cannon, answering cannon peal.
  The Austrian ranks are mown, and soon re-
   veal
The battle's havoc, and a King's defeat ;
  Flags flaunting sway, as cheers of vict'ry steal
Upon the air, with sadder sounds replete,
Where dying heroes fell, and conquering heroes
   meet.

Austria's Imperial Guard gives way,
  .For two thirds of its numbers strew the
   ground ;

And as the beams of light grow faint and gray,
  The heavens reëcho the exultant sound
  Which rises from the victors ; far around
Are seen War's crushed and bleeding victims ;
    far
The steps of the retreating foe resound :
The twilight fades, and now the evening star
Beholds the victor grieving o'er the field of war.

CANTO THE THIRD.

"On! to Austria's Capitol!
Batter down each frowning wall!"
Cried the French; and on they sped
Over crushed and mangled dead.
Naught could stay th' impetuous mass;
Height ne'er rose they dare not pass;
Ran no river, stood no town,
They'd not cross, or batter down.
Bullets could not stop their course,
Batteries were useless force;
And ere long Vienna's spires
  Rose distinct to view;
And her walls were wrapped in fires
  As the conflict grew;
Wrapped in fires which fiercely spread,
'Till the coward Francis fled [1]
Leaving, in his sore dismay,
To the victor's clemency,
His frail child, who suffering lay.
Strange the fate which, later, led
  To the throne of Charlemagne,
This same princess, to be wed
  With the man whose mighty name

[1] The Austrian Emperor fled from his Capitol on the approach of Napoleon's victorious army, leaving his child, Maria Louisa, who lay sick at the time.

Changed at once a nation's fate,
And whose armies, at the gate
Of her burning city, wait
'Till it shall capitulate.
Proud Vienna! what a fall!
Over Austria's Capitol,
Floats the same tri-colored sign,
Waving o'er the gleaming Rhine.
Thus Napoleon gloriously
Crowned his arms with victory;
Europe trembled at his nod
As he swayed the iron rod
Of his justice o'er the lands,
And with his devoted bands
Drove before him princes, kings,
Emperors, and lesser things;
Reaping from the land along,
Many a blessing, many a song, —
Sung by those who feared defeat
Was a word with woes replete.
Born upon an isle afar,
Guided by his natal Star,
Rising solely by his will,
And his own unrivaled skill,
With two Empires at his feet,
Where I ask, and where, repeat,
Rose so great a man before —
One who should be honored more?
France has dealt an awful blow,
But has not yet crushed her foe;
Many a shriek has yet to rise
To the gloomy, northern skies;

Many a loyal heart must be
Stilled amid strange misery;
Much of life-blood, flowing free,
Yet must. color Danube's waves;.
Thousands, fit for heroes' graves,
    Yet must writhe beneath the tread
Of red-crested, ruthless Mars,
And the weary, watching stars,
    Yet must gleam on fields of dead,
Ere fair France with peacefulness
Her devoted sons can bless.

WAGRAM.

I.

The night had been a night of fearful gloom;
  On Wagram's field a mighty host had lain;
But scarcely will red Ruin e'er find room
  The coming day, upon that trampled plain,
  To pile his ghastly heaps of human slain.

II.

Through all the night, into the gray of morn,
 . From post to post Napoleon headlong sped,
With eagle eye to watch, though ne'er to scorn
  The humblest soldier, or his humbler bed; —
  For warm his heart for those his wisdom led.

III.

As morning broke unceasing din arose,
  For .lines were formed, and batteries planted high;

Each soldier grasps his arms — no more repose —
  War claims each thought, and softer feelings fly ;
  Stern grows each brow, and stern each flashing
    eye.

IV.

Yet in those bands how many a noble heart
  Beat faster for the loved ones far away !
But battle-fields are not for tears to start !
  At least when heroes hasten to the fray ;
  These must be stern — 'tis those at home must
    pray.

V.

A mighty host ! three hundred thousand men,
  Each at another aiming for a blow !
What human power that awful tide can stem ?
  Or who can hope, 'mid general overthrow,
  To breast its billows as they wildly flow ?

VI.

O, never yet hath pen been made to tell,
  Or pencil paint, in colors that can vie
With those which many there saw but too well,
  The sad, the terrible reality
  O'er which, that day, was bent the murky sky.

VII.

Napoleon formed his lines ; and through the smoke
  With which the batteries, far and near, began
The atmosphere with sulphury smell to choke,
  With awful might he executes each plan,
  Nerves, guides, and singles out each man.

VIII.

Upon one move the Empire's fate is cast :
The Austrian centre must be pierced ; and he,
The hero of the .fight, — whose name has passed
Down history's pages, crowned with victory, —
McDonald ! thine the daring task must be !

IX.

Along they thunder ; men of iron will,
Braced by the cannon at each flank and rear,
And headed by McDonald, dark and still,
Who never felt one thrill of human fear,
And loved his land with loving most sincere.

X.

On, on they sweep ! and mark the path they make !
Like one vast swath the dead are left behind !
Mark how the Austrian batteries rake
Those solid ranks of men, 'till earth is lined
With heroes. Heaven should weep if 'twere not
blind.

XI.

At times the line will stagger — waver — reel,
As that tremendous fire cuts down its head ;
Then gaze again, and every man seems steel,
"Till he, too, sinks upon the mangled dead,
And lies there crushed beneath his comrades'
tread.

XII.

Those brave ranks reel, and now McDonald's voice
Rings o'er the din. He waves his hand, — all
glance

Towards yonder height, where stands their Chief.
　" Rejoice,
And on ! ere yet the Old Guard shall advance,
For ye, my braves, can save the flags of France ! "

XIII.

It is enough ; these words, this thought inspires ;
　They shout, " Napoleon ! France ! " and ere the
　　sound
Dies 'mid the thunder, lo ! the Austrian fires
　Fall harmless on the gory, trampled ground : —
　They've pierced the centre, and the foe lie dead
　　around.

XIV.

With *sixteen thousand* men that charge began.
　Now look along the land with life-blood red
But *sixteen hundred* stand there, man for man ;
　So well have flown those awful bolts of lead, —
　Ten out of every eleven lie dead.

XV.

O, brave McDonald ! France may justly boast
　Thy greatness. Joined with Napoleon's name
And Wagram's, thine grows bright among the host
　Of those whose deeds, though great, by yours were
　　tame,
　And blazons France with an immortal fame.

For the seventh time France was free ;[1]
For the seventh time victory

[1] " The *first* coalition against France was concluded between

Crowned her banners. Austria
At Napoleon's mercy lay,
Taught by loss of life and power,
Woe 's the. day, and woe 's the hour,

Austria and Prussia, to check the progress of the French Revolution, February 7, 1792.

"The *second* coalition was that of 1793, in which Germany declared war against Republican France, and was joined by Portugal, Naples, Tuscany, and the Pope.

"The *third* coalition was formed at St. Petersburg, between
England, Russia, and Austria, September 28, 1795. Napoleon
was then just emerging into manhood. He drove the English
from Toulon ; repelled the invading Austrians, and shattered
the third coalition by the tremendous blows he struck in the
Italian campaign. England, from her inaccessible island, con-
tinued the war, and organized a *fourth* coalition against France,
with Russia, Austria, Naples, and Turkey, December 28, 1798.
The ties of this coalition Napoleon severed with his sword at
Marengo. Hardly had one short year passed ere England again
declared war, and formed the *fifth* coalition, April 18, 1803, between England, Russia, Austria, and Prussia. At Ulm and
Austerlitz Napoleon again repelled his assailants, and again
compelled them to sheathe the sword. But hardly had the
blade entered the scabbard before it was again drawn, and
fiercely brandished as England, Russia, Prussia, Saxony, and
other minor powers formed a *sixth* coalition, and marched upon
France. Napoleon met them at Jena and Auerstadt, at Eylau
and Friedland, and disciplined them into good behavior. The
peace of Tilsit was signed July 9, 1807. Not two years had
passed before England had organized a *seventh* coalition with
the insurgents of Spain and Portugal, and with Austria. On
the blood-stained field of Wagram, Napoleon detached Austria
from this alliance. The peace of Vienna was signed. October
14, 1809."

4

When insulted France arises,
And with marches and surprises,
Forces, from her strongest foe,
Peace at one tremendous blow.
Gladly Francis, in his shame,
To the peace affixed his name ;
And weary Europe smiled once more,
And chanted hymns from shore to shore ;
But England, ocean-bound, decrees
That France shall never be at peace,
Till on her throne a Bourbon sit,
And "*plebeian generals*" bow to it.

. . . .

Earthly power is often pain,
Causing tears to fall like rain ;
For, upon the nation's sky,
Soon Napoleon's practiced eye
Could discern, as clouds are seen
When the air seems most serene,
One small spot, which threatened fast,
  Though no larger than a hand,
All the sky to overcast,
  And to shroud again the land
In the gloom which gathers o'er
Lands made dark with human gore.

Love must make his sacrifice ;
Interest must sunder ties
Strong as were those words of law,
Which the sons of Israel saw

'Graved by Moses on a stone
When he talked with God alone.
Thrones and crowns need heirs ; and he
Who hath raised fair France to be
Great and glorious, from her shame
Would perpetuate his name,
And by an illustrious bride
Win this boon, so long denied.

DIVORCE OF JOSEPHINE.

In a palace hall met a royal crowd ;
   There were kings, and queens, and men of state ;
There was pomp and glitter, and two heads
      bowed, —
   Low bowed to the awful blow of fate.
O'er every face seemed a shade of gloom,
   To many a lip arose a sigh,
And the dazzling light of that gorgeous room
   All felt, at a glance, most painfully.

The monarch, dressed in his robes of state,
   With pallid brow and wandering eye,
And a bloodless lip which told the weight
   Of the sorrow borne so silently,
'Gainst a marble pillar leaned calm and still,
   And sadly gazed on the silent throng,
As the words were read, which, spite his will,
   Took from him her he had loved so long.

And the Empress sat with her head bowed down,
  And face as white as the winter's snow ;
O, who can tell how that glittering crown
  Wrung her tender heart with its weight of woe !
Alas ! that a woman e'er must give
  Her heart's best love on the shrine of fame ;
For the two in her bosom cannot live, —
  The *bliss of love* and the *pride of name.*

The words are read, and the deed is done ;
  The widowed Empress has left the room ;
The tears of her daughter are flowing fast,
  Her son is wrapped in unconscious gloom.
And the husband ! he of the royal will,
  And deeds which have filled a world with awe !
His sore heart bleeds, but his lips are dumb,
  For the people's will is the people's law.[1]

          .   .   .   .

When the stars came out, the Emperor sought
  His lonely room and his vacant bed ;
His brow was ashen with bitter thought, —
  He entered the chamber as one were dead ;
But he scarcely had lain himself to rest
  When, sobbing and overcome with woe,
The Empress slowly, with loosened dress,
  Entered the room, her head bowed low.

[1] "Though Josephine was loved as an amiable sovereign,
who represented goodness and grace by the side of might, the
French desired, with regard for her, another marriage which
should give heirs to the Empire. Nor did they confine themselves to wishes on the subject." — THIERS.

A moment more, and Napoleon caught
His weeping wife to his heaving breast, —
There, clasped in a faithful, fond embrace,
We leave the two to that last, sad rest.

. . . .

The bonds of law are broken;
The farewell words are spoken;
Napoleon sits alone
On his grand, unrivaled throne;
But a bitter, burning pain,
Agony, intense as vain,
Colors all his future sky
With an awful brilliancy;
Awful with the voiceless woe
Hearts unfilled forever know;
Brilliant to his longing glance
With the fate he paints for France,
When the cloud of war no more
Shall its crimson rain outpour.
Thus with eager hopefulness,
Does he look at last for rest,
When he shall have wed with one
Young and fair, and royal born, —
Daughter of the Austrian king.
She it was whom Interest chose
For Napoleon's future spouse,
Peace unto the lands to bring.

Bonny France then glowed with light;
From each valley and each height,
Bonfires blazed, and music's clang
On the breezes rose and rang;

Universal shoutings sent
To the echoing firmament,
Told the people joyed to know
There now seemed an end to woe.
Mirth and music, pride and power,
Hastened on each lagging hour,
And the French, o'erjoyed, excited,
Cheered for nations thus united.
All seems gladness; but two hearts
Every strain of music starts.
Josephine, in palace pent,
Prays with dim eyes upward bent
To the cloudless firmament;
While the Emperor, in state,
Meets his bride, accepting fate;
Feeling all that dazzling show,
Through which calmly he must go, —
Bitterest mockery of his woe.

.   .   .   .

England, still, with hatred fanned
Each unrest in every land, .
Pouring through insurgent Spain
Armies, till each height and plain
Rang with many a martial strain.
In the north war seemed at rest;
One had hardly dared to guess
That the sky, which seemed so clear,
Held a tempest most severe.

.   .   .   .

Hear ye not the clang of bells
Which upon the soft air swells?

Hear ye not exultant notes
As the cannon's thunder floats
Forth upon the trembling air?
Do ye ask what means that cheer
Rising to heaven's lofty dome?
There is born a king for Rome.
These glad sounds announce his birth
To the monarchs of the earth.
Well, ah, well! I would that he
Linked more close to Austria
France, that war no more might be.
For, alas! clouds quickly spread
From the Northland overhead,
And their muttering thunders pour
Through the skies of France once more.
Russia has awoke to life,
And is eager for the strife,
Urged by England's gold and power,
To "let loose the dogs of war."
Weary, worn, yet full of pride,
France prepares to stem the tide.
Judging from her past career
She hath *now* no cause to fear.
Quickly then she forms her lines;
Death to all! ere she resigns
That brave heart, whose throbbings make
Europe's gathered despots quake.

Gallop columns; marshal bands;
Pushing toward the hostile lands,
Shaking many a kingdom's base
In the world's bewildered face.

Critics wonder at the stride
Of Napoleon's injured pride.
Alexander should have known
He'd not tamely be o'erthrown ;
For his troops were fond as brave,
Nor recked of life their land to save ;
And now they felt he needed them
Some terrific tide to stem.
This alone sufficed to rouse
Stalwart men from every house ;
This alone sufficed, when they,
Snug within their quarters, lay
By the Volga's shore, to say,
" Soldiers ! there 's a foe to brave !
Filled ye not full many a grave
With our foes, at red Marengo ?
Hurled ye not your thousands low
At Austerlitz and Friedland ?
Are ye not that gallant band
Which, on Wagram's bloody plain,
Strewed the ground with foemen slain ? "
Spoke their chief such words, and lo !
Forth those massive columns go,
Heedless both of cold and snow,
While the world looks on with eyes
Wide and widening with surprise,
That Napoleon should thus dare
" Beard the lion in his lair ; "
Marching with a whirlwind's start
Into Russia's very heart.
Thus, obedient to his will,
Onward move his armies, till

Russian plains and Russian skies
Meet the anxious soldiers' eyes.
Onward still, until in sight
Moscow's spires are gleaming bright.
'Long the Russian lines have fled
  Those who should have staid to meet,
And in many a home, instead,
  Desolation reigns complete, —
Desolation, silent, chill,
Seeming harbinger of ill.
But unto those weary men —
Those brave, uncomplaining men —
Food and rest most tempting are;
And they gladly shelter them
In the city of the Czar.
But not long; behold! the sky
Glows with startling brilliancy.
" Ho, there! comrades! fire! fire! fire!
See! the city is on fire!" —
Every moment flames leap higher —
" Where 's the Corporal? find him! call!
Save him, though the skies should fall!"
Ah! *his* eye had caught the glare
Ere the creaking, frosty air
Quivered to that lusty cry,
Echoed by the starry sky;
And his mighty mind had grasped
All the dangers to be passed
'Mid that wild and hostile clime,
Ere those loyal hearts had time
To suspect the maddened foe
Meant to fire their city so,   .

And to lay its grandeur low,
That *they* might find graves of snow.

BURNING OF MOSCOW.

In the chill and gloom of the still night air
There suddenly rose up a torch-light glare ;
Steadily, grandly, the flame stretched high,
'Till it seemed to dance on the northern sky ;
And it gathered strength as it shot along,
As a singer's voice at the close of song ;
And it gathered brilliancy, too, and might,
Till the whole heavens glowed with the sea of light.
The furious flames, with their breath of fire,
Seemed one vast, extending, funeral pyre ;
Palace and cottage, each hut and hall,
The noble's couch, and the peasant's stall,
The beauty's satins, the beggar's rags,
Most costly jewels, and waving flags,
Spices and fruits, and all things grand,
Served but to heat up the flame-licked land.
And the flames grew fiercer, until a sea
Of the rolling fire surged brilliantly ;
And the sweeping winds, with their frozen breath,
Rushed to the warmth and were burned to death ;
Or howled, with a piteous clamor, out
To the still free breezes which roamed about ;
While the terrible heat, for miles around,
Withered, and scorched, yea, and blistered the
      ground.
Poet or painter ne'er dared to dream
Of aught that could equal the strange, wild scene.

Far out in the shadow, o'er plains of snow,
At times there trembles a savage glow,
As echo answers the ringing crash
Of the flaming towers as they downward dash ;
Or, like wandering meteors, shoot through air,
And light up each nook with a fearful glare ;
And the form of man, like an insect small,
Crouches down, low down by many a wall,
While the flames roll on in their awful might,
Till they force the shivering wretch to flight ;
And the murmur of friend, as he seeks the snow,
Is echoed in groans by the burning foe.

And thus they writhed, and shrieked, and died ;
And the fire-fiend swayed his sceptre wide,
And grinned o'er the city's burning pride ;
For swiftly the pride of the city fell,
Engulfed in those crimson waves of hell.

Napoleon viewed, with a mournful eye,
That scene of surpassing sublimity ;
For he felt, when the flames of Moscow rose,
They were deadlier far than all human foes ;
And he knew, when the burning city fell,
That his army's doom was inevitable.
But the hungry flames, for the lack of food,
Or by will of God, were at length subdued,
And the French were left, 'mid the drifting snow,
Outside of the place where had stood Moscow.

Conquering French ! Yet forced to go
Through a dreary realm of snow.

Lords of what ?   A city's grave,
    Desolation, want, and woe ;
Vanquished not, yet suffering still
    All the ills of overthrow.
Sullen, proud, reluctant, they
Turn about to force their way
Through a frozen wilderness,
Followed closely by distress,
And a foe, which, now and then,
Pounced upon those weary men ;
And which gathered savage strength
As the army trailed its length,
As compactly as could be,
O'er the desolate country.
On the rear, the left, the right,
Some must stand and breast the fight,
While the rest, with measured tread,
Hurriedly march on ahead.
But the foe they dreaded most
Was not any human host ;
Frost and famine thinned their bands
As though culled by demon hands ;
Some lay down with stupid stare
In the depths of frosty air ;
Others, wrapped in bloody shrouds,
Fell beneath the falling clouds
Of drifting snow and driving sleet.
All along that sad retreat
The dead lay 'neath the living's feet,
Mingled with the vast array
Of the wealth they flung away,

When, too weary more to bear,
They had yielded to despair,
Or alone had sought to save
Themselves from a foreign grave.
Shrank not then Napoleon's soul,
As those living horrors roll,
Fast and thick, on every side,
O'er his mighty army's pride?
No. With iron firmness then
He infused into his men
Something of his own strong hope,
Giving strength with Death to cope.
Scarce one murmuring voice arose
Though they felt so many woes. —
For too feeble is the pen
To immortalize such men;
Men, who, daring danger, death,
Men, who, yielding up their breath,
Gloried in this great bequest,
Cheered their chief, and sank to rest.
Thus they moved, blest with the thought
   That they'd reach a place at last,
Where a shelter might be had,
   And perhaps a good repast.
But as on they boldly strode
O'er the pathless, trackless road,
News was sent, each place of rest
Was with Russian troops infest; ·
And, that, freezing, faint, and weak,
Not yet were their woes complete.
They had yet to onward press
Through a frozen wilderness,

Blocked up oft with deadly foes,
And the still descending snows.
Pierced with cold, with hunger faint,
Still they would not make complaint;
Still they formed their lines, and met
Russian ranks, with lips firm set,
And with hands as strong to deal
   Death and ill by ball or blow,
As when erst their cannon's peal
   Shook that startled land of snow.

Still, with Ney to guard the rear,
   (Rightly named the bravest brave, —
He who never dreamed of fear,)
   Thousands found a nameless grave.
Many times the savage foe
Separated with quick blow
His brave squadrons, and each host
Seemed to each forever lost;
Then, with most tremendous might,
Each would close the foe in fight,
And through bullets reunite;
'Till that long retreat at last,
With its awful woes, was passed;
And brave Ney the Niemen o'er,
Fired the last shot on its shore,
Then, with tears and tenderness,
Turned his soldiers to embrace.

O, how scanty was the band
Who beheld their native land;

Veterans, who had hurled the foe
To the dust upon Marengo,
Dreamless slept 'mid northern snow.
Marshals who had watched " the sun
Of Austerlitz," the battle won,
Reposed within a foreign grave
O'er which the French flag ne'er might wave ;
While, to every home in France,
Sorrow stalked in swift advance,
Making cheeks and lips all pale
With its terribly sad tale.

On one gray and gloomy night,
    When o'er Paris silence lay,
Chilly as the northern snows
    Falling softly far away,
When around the Tuileries
    Darkness seemed to gather thick,
And the Empress had retired
    To her chamber, sad and sick ;
Suddenly the door swung wide,
And a man stood at her side ;
'Twas the Emperor, back again
From that terrible campaign.
Briefly then he did relate
The story of his army's fate,
And how that gallant army then
Was a few, brave, famished men,
Struggling homeward, all the way
Holding countless foes at bay.
Then he kindly soothes her fright,
And betakes himself, that night,

To preparing for the blow
Which he deems his savage foe
Will attempt. The old and young,
'Round whom wives and children clung,
Heard the summons, and with tears
   Buckled on the trusty blade,
Kissed dear lips with loving fears,
   Lips of trusting wife and maid,
Then with brave hearts beating high,
Hastened forth unfalteringly.

And thus once more the chief of France
Against her foes makes swift advance,
Determined to oppose and fight
The front, before they all unite.
On Lutzen's plains the armies meet,
And there those raw recruits repeat
The deeds of veterans ; shot and shell,
And sabre-strokes, which on them fell,
Left those brave ranks unswerved, though deep
The awful missiles through them sweep.
'Gainst fearful odds they battle on ;
Till, lo ! the victory they have won ;
And the proud Allies turn and flee
To meet their friends dejectedly.

For Dresden now the French push on,
While despots' faces grow more wan.
They dare not meet, in hurried fight,
This man of such resistless might,
Who from his subjects, at one call,
Could marshal bands to meet them all.

They needs must gather greater force
Before they prosecute their course ;
They needs must call into their van
That treacherous, vacillating man, —
The Austrian Emperor, who could turn
Against his child : the world will learn
That kith and kin of royal blood
Are sought, or fought, as seemeth good.

With support like this, so strong,
Hesitate they now not long ;
And they form in kingly pride
Dresden's frowning walls beside
And before, to " fight and die "
Swearing, so each Frenchman lie
Buried 'neath the ruins there,
Or surrenders in despair.

Love nor courage could prevail
'Gainst that storm of leaden hail
From their swarming enemies,
Thick as are the sands of seas ;
And the bravest were dismayed
At the scene they then surveyed.
Allies of Napoleon's power
Coldly turned in that dark hour ;
And as horrors multiplied,
All save one forsook his side ;
One, the Saxon King, stood by ;
And together they defy

5

England, Russia, Austria, Spain,
Prussia, Sweden, Denmark ; — vain
Was human might to stand
'Gainst this terribly strong band.
Minor powers soon flock along,
Till Napoleon, though still strong,
Seems as if ordained to be
Completely crushed with treachery.
Still the soldiers, desperate,
Battle fiercely with their fate ;
Gath'ring round their chief, they swear
By the past all must beware !
Fifty thousand anxious men
Clamor to be led out then,
Where three hundred thousand wait
Each French home to desolate.
Every soldier longs to prove
How devoted is his love
For his chief, his Emperor,
Forced to this unequal war.

Well such love Napoleon prized,
But he would not sacrifice
Life and limb, to nothing gain
Save a heap of human slain.
Hunted down, and caged at last,
    What can love avail ?
Blood and want have thickened fast,
    And all efforts fail
To beat back the countless foe, —
Moulding France for future woe.

Marshals, soldiers, all have fought
With the might despair has wrought.
But, alas ! relentless Fate
Bids Napoleon 'abdicate.
Fortune's star has sunk, and now
Fortune's favorite can but bow.
   Destiny has raised him high,
Destiny now brings him low ;
   (But upon life's future sky
There is bent a brilliant bow ;
'Tis the promise of a name
Crowned with an immortal fame.)
Such the thoughts with which he strives
   To endure his overthrow :
Throned upon a nation's love,
   Still to Elba he must go,
And upon that lonely isle
Wait for Fate again to smile.

'Mid his fallen fortunes, where
Is the one should soothe his care ?
   Where art *thou*, imperial bride,
As *he* seeks an exile's home ?
   Doomed by despots, far and wide,
To an isle 'mid ocean's foam,
O'er the billows of the sea,
Naught to cheer, not even *thee !*
   Ah ! that woman for her pride
Should desert and leave alone
Him who when his life was bright,
She had clung to, wrong or right !

But I joy to paint a scene
  To redeem my sex from shame;
Turn to faithful Josephine,
  And with reverence speak her name.
Love like hers, in that dark hour,
  Shone with royal purity;
She had shared Napoleon's power,
  She would bear his misery,
If no other deemed her place
By her lord a queenly grace.
Tender were her words of cheer,
Penned with anxious hope and fear,
Asking, with devotion great,
If she might not share his fate.[1]

[1] In her letter to Napoleon after his banishment to Elba, Josephine says : " Now only can I calculate the whole extent of the misfortune of having beheld my union with you dissolved by law. Now do I indeed lament being no more than your friend, who can but mourn over a misfortune great as it is unexpected. Ah, sire! why can I not fly to you! Why can I not give you the assurance that exile has no terrors save for vulgar minds ; and that, far from diminishing a sincere attachment, misfortune imparts to it a new force. I have been upon the point of quitting France to follow your footsteps, and to consecrate to you the remainder of an existence which you so long embellished. A single motive restrains me, and that you may divine. If I learn that I am the only one who will fulfill her duty, nothing shall detain me, and I will go to the only place where, henceforth, there can be happiness for me, since I shall be able to console you when you are isolated and unfortunate. Say but the word, and I depart. Adieu, sire ! Whatever I would add would still be too little. It is no longer by *words* that my sentiments for you are to be proved, and for *actions* your consent is necessary."

What will not *true* woman bear
   For the object of her love !
Want, woe, wrong, and e'en despair,
   Ne'er her steadfast truth can move ;
Thus the name of Josephine
Glorifies this gloomy scene.

Deep anxiety and grief
For the nation's chosen chief —
(Not *her husband;* she could ne'er
Call him now by words so dear ;
Never call *him* husband ! O,
Heaviest weight of human woe !
That another one should claim
That beloved, illustrious name !
And should rest in bliss where she
Once was clasped so tenderly,
While the world, with harshness rife,
Names *that* woman as *his wife !*)
Soon from life gave her relief ;
Yes, regret and gnawing pain
Soon made human longing vain.
Death advanced with rapid stride
To the great, good Empress' side,
And, in an imperious voice,
Called her from her brave soul's choice,
While the monarchs of the land
Knelt, and reverent, kissed her hand,
Listening to the words her lips
Breathed from out her life's eclipse —
Fondest words those lips could say,
" Dear Napoleon ! Isle of Elba ! "

Thus her spirit rose from this
To a world of perfect bliss;
To a place of loftier state,
There her love and lord to wait;
There, secure from earthly strife,
To keep vigil o'er his life.

. . . .

Poor, crushed France! o'errun with foes,
Trembling, bleeding 'neath their blows,
Now thou mayst take thy repose.
Take your rest! — him you adore
Exiled to a distant shore!
Branded *tyrant*, *despot*, all
To extenuate his fall!
Named *usurper*, when the voice
Of a mighty nation's choice
Raised him up, and placed him high
On a seat of royalty!
With your homes by foes invest,
And your Emperor exiled, rest!

CANTO THE FOURTH.

O, WAVE-WASHED Elba! to your shore
Stout ships earth's greatest monarch bore.
A few tried friends had asked, and won,
The right to share his island home.
The people met, with outstretched hands,
Napoleon, and his faithful bands;
For greater now he seemed to be
Thus doomed to lone captivity.
Forced by outnumbering foes, alone,
To abdicate his peerless throne,
His fame was spreading far and wide,
And praise was his on every side.
The people knew he was their friend,
And groaned at such an unjust end;
But iron despotism swayed
All Europe, and they sank dismayed.
Yet still a murmur, scarcely heard,
Among the masses ever stirred;
Distracted Europe could not quell
The storm which gathered fast and well;
It could not still the deep unrest
Which throbbed within the common breast;
And thus the name of this one man,
   Securely guarded o'er the sea,
Struck coldly to the despots' hearts
   Like sound of direst prophecy.

Backed by keen swords in stalwart hands,
They looked with terror o'er the lands,
And glancing o'er the Great Sea's foam,
They cried in fear, "Is he at home?"

How could one man, nor troops, nor power,
Disturb so well their safest hour?
Why should they tremble, as, alone,
Afar from France, his army, throne,
This man, though of gigantic mind,
To their decree himself resigned?
Ah! well they knew despotic power
  Was trampling down the mighty *right;*
And thus they feared that, any hour,
  He with the people might unite.

Prophetic fear! when ten months fled
Poor France upraised her humbled head;
With wild eyes wide, and pleading voice,
She calls, "Come back! O chief of choice!"
With throbbing heart Napoleon hears,
Scarce able to suppress his tears,
His bosom thronged with hopes and fears.
Not long he waits: "Forthwith," says he,
"I'll be upon the bounding sea;
O, bonny France! my suffering land!
Thy helm of state I'll grasp in hand."

He reached his native shore ere they
Who feared him most his steps could stay.
His faithful followers were those
Who life with him in exile chose; —

Six hundred men, whose bravery
But equaled their fidelity;
And homeward now they followed him,
   With faith which evermore survived;
They landed, and with bulletins
   Announced *the Emperor* had arrived.
Then everywhere throughout the land,
The people rose with cap in hand,
And smiled and shouted, wept and sung,
As though a jubilee 'd begun:
They knelt to him, they kissed his hand,
And wildest joy swept o'er the land;
From shore to city, town to town,
   He hurries on, and none oppose, —
This, this alone proves his renown,
   And stops the mouths of lying foes.
Whatever troops were sent to check
His onward march, as soon as met
They join and swell that mighty sea
Of joyful love and loyalty.
The brave Old Guard, the Cuirassiers,
Gens d'armes, and even bronzéd tars,
The peasantry, the people all,
Embrace "the little Corporal."
Was this a monster, whose delight
Was seas of blood and deeds of night?
Was this a despot, giving naught
But curses as his subjects fought?
Was this a fiend whose courser's feet
Pranced firm through red blood fetlock deep?
Was this a man within whose breast
No mercy e'er was known to rest?

One who oppressed and slaughtered men
As Heaven held no recording pen?
Alas, historians! human fiend
With love like this was never screened.

They followed him with shout and song,
As, conqueror-like, he passed along;
From Cannes to Lyons, from Grenoble,
Each rank of true hearts 'gan to double.
Decrees he issued full of pride:
"No blood must flow on either side!"
He would not have a throne which caused
One drop of French blood to be lost.
Rejoicing Paris opened wide
Her arms, as eagerly she cried,
"O, welcome! welcome! father, come!
Your children bid you welcome home!"
They caught him in their arms, and bore
Him proudly to the palace door;[1]
Fair hands flung wreaths, sweet lips breathed
        song,
The crowd surged eagerly along;
They placed him on the throne, and then
Proclaimed him mightiest of men.
"Vive l'Empereur!" "Vive l'Empereur!"
In thunder tones rose everywhere.

O, wondrous march! The Bourbon King
Had failed like any useless thing;

[1] "The moment the carriage stopped, he was seized by those
next the door, borne aloft in their arms, amid deafening cheers,
through a dense and brilliant throng." — *Alison.*

His friends, or those he deemed were such,
Had sought the man they loved so much ;
And thus the hope of Bourbon power,
The hope of kings, fell in an hour.

Triumphant march ! the world will ne'er
  Behold its like again, I ween ;
Napoleon's rank is proven clear
  By this, as yet, unrivaled scene.
He sat upon his throne once more,
And despots rose from shore to shore ;
They who had trod with savage pride
The people down, now rose and cried,
" It is not well ; up, kings, we must
Crush down this tyrant to the dust !
He threatens kingdoms to o'erthrow ;
Brand him an outcast, and a foe !
We must not rest until his fall, —
So gather, gather, one and all ! "

Well may ye ask the reason why
All Europe doomed this man to die ?
Alas ! he fought with all his might
Armed in the panoply of *right;*
He battled for *the people,* they
Who loved such sovereigns to obey.
The allied powers had forced on them
  The Bourbon rule, — which they despise ;
And thus, to free themselves from it,
  They welcomed any sacrifice ;

They welcomed danger, welcomed war,
With their beloved Emperor.

Again, alas! the whirr of war
Came rolling inward from afar;
Gigantic were the plans to end
The life of this, the people's friend.
The life of France and his were one, —
Dethrone *him*, France was left undone.
Left to internal strife, without
Her greedy foes would throng about,
And, crushing her within their toils,
Would quarrel e'en about the spoils.
Yet gathered, swiftly gathered they
Whose thirst for blood no right could stay;
Each prince, each king, with all his might
Prepared for this tremendous fight, —
This trampling down of sovereign right.

Ah! well Napoleon once had said,
"When all is done, and I am dead,
Great Britain will regret, and sigh
Because of Belgium's victory;
That mighty northern power, the Czar,
Will stretch his sceptre quite too far
To suit her greedy, grasping mind:" —
But then, the blind did lead the blind.

How felt Napoleon in that hour,
When battling Europe's banded power?
O, shrank not he to face, *alone*,
    That awful tempest rolling near?

Not he ; he rose as he had known
  No thrill, no thought of human fear,
And with supremest majesty
Bade France to form for victory.
The "plains of Mars" shook 'neath the feet
Of those who hurried him to meet.
Each soldier, shouting in the din,
Receives the eagle given to him,
And vows while life and strength remain
That symbol shall not bear a stain.
His chieftain's words he scarcely hears
Above the crashing, deafening cheers,
But firm he grasps, with love and pride,
The gift for which so soon he died.

In this *ninth* great coalition,
Bent on one tremendous mission,
First rose England, in the van
Placing every fighting man ;
Next came Russia, and her Czar
Armed his millions for the war ;
Sweden then joined in with those
Whom before she named as foes ;
Portugal, with coward Spain,
Lent her aid to crush again
Him whose noblest feelings made
Europe 'gainst him stand arrayed.
Prussia armed her subjects, too,
In the gladdened despots' view ;
Italy and Austria
Eagerly rushed to the fray,

Joined with minor powers, who, weak,
Think the *strongest* side to seek
Is the *best;* it may be so,
But my heart would whisper, no !
France stood proudly up, *alone,*
To defend her crown and throne,
Nerved by him whom naught could move
Save his faithful subjects' love.
Grandly then, amid the gloom
(Deep as that which shrouds a tomb),
  Which each moment·deeper grew,
Towered the *Statesman,* who foresaw
That the nation needed law,
  And while forming armies, drew
  Master-statutes, just and new ;
Laws which startled with their force
Those who watched his wondrous course.[1]
Yet, despite this weight of care,
Lo ! he found time to repair
To the lovely, hallowed scene,
Where, agone, with Josephine,
He had passed the hours most sweet
Of a life with good replete.
There we find the warrior, *man,*
  Filled with loving tenderness,
Which, in all his after life,
  Dark with ills, was never less.
There he scrupled not to shed
Bitter tears above his dead.

[1] Said Madame de Staël of the additional acts to the Constitution of the State : "They are all that is wanted for France."

Aye, his very soul did melt
As upon each spot he dwelt,
Calling up from out the past
Her who loved him to the last;
Grieving o'er each look and tone
Which forevermore had flown.
Fame is e'en a mighty thing,
But 'tis love doth crown man king;
And Napoleon, *greatest* seen,
Was when mourning Josephine.
Emperor, statesman, warrior, man,
To admire, refuse, who can?
Mighty Emperor, statesman deep,
Warrior great, yet *man* to weep!
Tender memories thrilling him,
Forth he goes amid the din.
Up his army sprang, as he
Were a very deity;
And again, as oft before,
Home was midst the battle's roar.

Scanty were his bands to meet
Those who fought for his defeat;
A million foes, with awful strides,
Were 'circling France on all her sides;
And each soldier knew full well
Shot and sabre-stroke must tell;
They must gain by zealousness
What they lacked in numbers less.
So they forward press to close
With the foremost of their foes,
Hoping, by determined blows

Quick and strong, to break the band
Gathering nearest at their hand.

Ah! Napoleon was aware,
Should his army be laid bare
To the millions all *united*,
That his hopes were surely blighted.
Thus he would attack the front,
As had often been his wont,
Then, before surprise subsided,
Other bands, as yet divided,
Would be left to him a prey,
Which he soon could sweep away.

What a scene! From every quarter,
Troops are marching to the slaughter;
O'er the land in clouds they sweep,
    Round the forest, back, and through,
Marshaling where the sunbeams creep
    Slanting over Waterloo;
There they halt, and wait their doom
In the most tempestuous gloom.

Out amid a storm of rain,
As unknowing human pain,
Or fatigue, or aught but will,
    Does Napoleon pace the ground
By a lantern's light, until
    All his troops are stationed 'round,
There to wait, in darkest night,
For the coming morning's light,
And the great decisive fight.

WATERLOO.

A Sabbath morning rose with gloom and mist,
  And clouds above, and miry earth beneath ;
And Nature looked as though she ne'er was kissed
  By aught of loveliness, but only grief.
O'er all the ground was spread the human grist,
  Which Mars had gathered from the world's great
    sheaf,
And which, within that awful, fated day,
Was to be ground, and thrown, as chaff, away.

Upon a gentle rise of trampled ground
  The English force was placed. A forest dense
Lay back behind, which echoed to the sound
  Of clanging drum, and all the roar intense
Which rose and rolled up to the blue profound,
  And throbbed and thrilled along man's inner
    sense,
Jarring and quivering through his soul's repose,
And drowning thought of battle's many woes.

Upon another rise, and parallel,
  The French were posted, cannon-shot from foe ;
Each had position chosen wondrous well
  That each might feel the other's crashing blow ;
And very soon and very fast it fell,
  The which so many heroes sank below.
Ere long the clouds left unobscured the sun,
As God moved them to see what there was done.
6

O'er what *was* seen the *angels* well may weep,
   Since even *man* cannot withhold a tear ;
In solid masses posted firm and deep,
   Unflinching, stern, and knowing naught of fear,
The French are formed. They deem the price is
      cheap
   If with their lives they save sweet France, so
      dear
That every drop of blood, like incense given,
Doth plead their pardon at the bar of Heaven.

At 'leven o'clock the carnage fierce begun :
   The French dashed headlong on the rock-firm
      foe ;
Up rose the smoke, which soon obscured the sun,
   And wrapped in gloom the charging hosts be-
      low,
Who, long before that sultry day was done,
   Lay down to sleep the sleep that all must
      know ;
While with wild charges, thunder, rattle, roar,
Battalions dashed like waves against a shore,

And batteries belched, and shells, exploding,
      shrieked,
   And still those men charged to the cannon's
      mouth,
While blood outpoured, and, red and horrid,
      streaked
   The plains from East to West, from North to
      South ;

And sabres, swinging high above all, reeked
    And dripped as rain arresting summer's drouth;
Rider and horse, while clanging drum and fife
Beat on the chàrge, impetuous, sought the strife.

The Iron Duke stood on a rise of ground
    And watched the movements of the mighty host;
To him the roar of battle was the sound
    Familiar to his ear, and loved the most;
Yet sad his heart, as now he gazed around,
    Lest that the hard fought field at last were
        lost;
So murmured he, with eyes upon the sun,
" O l would to God that night or Blucher 'd come l"

And Blucher came, and the exhausted band
    Of brave, proud Frenchmen, who, with flashing
        eye,
Behold the Prussians spread out fresh and grand
    O'er the green slope, believe them *Destiny.*
They glance beneath — *their comrades pile the
    land* —
Then to their Emperor, and resolve *to die:*
He sits there calm, and counting every chance
Which now is left to save the life of France.

Few, O, how few! and yet no sign of fear
    Is seen to glance across his sallow cheek;
Along the line there rose a thrilling cheer
    As he surveyed their ranks, now thinned and
        weak;

Yet lips were firm, and eyes were flashing clear,
  As if to say, *The Old Guard now must speak !*
They stood aloof with bosoms beating high, —
They ne'er had moved but 'twas to victory.

In solid masses, firm, and fierce, and deep,
  They form behind impetuous Marshal Ney;
Then quick, with savage vengeance, on they sweep
  O'er piles of dead which block their awful way.
All sounds, as in expectant stillness, sleep,
  As every eye turns on that grand array
Of fearless men, who march through seas of gore,
The cannon, loaded muzzle-deep, before.

On, on they strode ; the British lines were still ;
  A stifling silence tells the awe of all
As down the slope, and up the other hill,
  They sternly go, to conquer, or to fall.
There was a moment's agitating thrill ;
  Then sped from every gun a flame-red pall,
And in the gaps those raking missiles tore
Unnumbered heroes fall, to rise no more.

They closed their ranks, and shouting, "Vive la
    France ! "
  With look of awful grandeur strode ahead,
Till lost unto Napoleon's anxious gaze,
  They pierced the British line with shattered
    head.
Alas for Justice! this, her only chance,
  Is lost for aye: *the grand Old Guard is dead !*

It sank in blood as Blucher's army came
With shouts exultant through the sea of flame.

. . . .

Who can paint, in colors true,
  That unparalleled retreat
From the world-famed Waterloo?
Struggling bands of weary men
  Sabered by pursuing foe,
Muttering curses of revenge
  As they sink beneath the blow;
Wounded horses rearing high,
Wounded men crawled off to die,
Bleeding squadrons rushing by —
  Wreck and ruin all complete.
Of the Old Guard there is left
  Just a remnant; in the rear
They protect the fugitives,
  And their worshipped Emperor.
They had seen their comrades go
For that charge upon the foe;
They beheld their fall, and swore
That for this rich blood should pour;
And when Blucher's savage men
To the last had driven them,
Like caged lions, fierce and hard,
Fought this gallant, glorious Guard;
'Till their very foes, admiring,
For a moment ceased their firing,
Offering, instead of slaughter,
To give honorable quarter.
Flashed each eye with royal fire,
Raised each arm a trifle higher,

Spoke these bleeding, brave defenders :
" *The Guard dies, but ne'er surrenders !*"
Then they plunge with savage pride
At their foes on every side.
'Twas enough ; one volley more
   And they all were swept away,
And their chieftain, far before,
   Gallops on his weary way,
Reaching Paris in the gloom
Of those awful *days of doom.*
Tumult now was everywhere,
Hands were red, and arms were bare,
Factions formed in every square.
The Chamber of the Deputies
Was perplexed with many fears :
Many said the Allies fought
   Only 'gainst Napoleon,
And if he would abdicate,
   Peace could easily be won.
This they said in fierce debate ;
But the loving people cried
Lustily on every side :
" Give us our arms ! our chieftain give !
And France in spite of all shall live ! "
Napoleon, pressed by adverse fate,
Deemed it wise to abdicate.
United, France could stem the tide,
But nations fall when they divide.

   .   .   .   .   .

Napoleon, citizen of France,
Beholds his country's foes advance ;

He has resigned his throne, yet they
Now make the insolent demand
That he shall leave his native land, —
  The war will cease with him away.
But whither can Napoleon go?
  His land is full of enemies,
  And hostile foes are on the seas,
Rejoicing at his overthrow.
Ah, whither? with an eagle eye
He scans the scene — then sorrowfully,
With royal pride and courtesy,
Seeks England's hospitality.

Then that whole great people rose,
  And with homage, deep and true,
Welcomed their illustrious guest;
  Well, aye, very well, *they* knew
That he was their friend; the best
That *the people* ever won
Anywhere beneath the sun.
Loud they shouted, long they sang,
Till the earth and heavens rang,
And the British ministry
Began to look uneasily
At such joyful demonstrations
Toward "the scourger of the nations;"
Then, ere long (I write with shame),
They malign his spotless name,
And in conclave called, agree
That a bare isle in the sea,
Far away in torrid zone,
Shall be given for his throne.

Wrong, unfit for heathen ages,
Thou art stamped on history's pages!
And so long as mind shall know
Right from wrong, or joy from woe,
Will it brand, with direst shame,
England's haught,[1] historic name.

So the British ministry
Sent him off across the sea.
  The *Northumberland,*
Stanch and stout to ride the wave,
Bore him to his island grave.
 Many begged his lot to share ;
  But a little band,
 Only, were allowed to care
 For him, when, in deep despair,
And with tearful eyes, he gave
 His last lingering look to France,
Sadly shouting o'er the wave,
" Farewell, France ! land of the brave ! "
 Then her hills, lost to his glance,
Sank amid the ocean's foam,
And he had nor land nor home.

 . . . .

Far away 'neath torrid skies
St. Helena's bleak rocks rise ;
Breezes from hot Afric's sand
Lash the waves upon its strand ;
Westward, waters infinite
Stretch away beyond the sight.

  [1] " Away, haught man ; thou art insulting me."
         SHAKESPEARE.

Bold and black against the sky
Loomed before Napoleon's eye,
This his prison rock, where he,
As a captive, left the sea ;
And within a low hut, where
There was lack of e'en pure air,
With his friends, the monarch saw
England's famous love of law (!)

Torn from France, the army, home,
There he was, and there, alone,
Did he bear with England's hate,
Which not yet had made his fate
          Sad and hard enough.
Dreary to him was each day,
   Dogged about by British sentry,
As he watched the ocean's spray.
   "General Bonaparte must be
Kept in sight," despatches say,
Lest on some propitious day
He launch out, in some frail skiff,
From some cove, hid by high cliff,
Over ocean, seeking for
More of fame, and more of war.
Poor, poor fools ! he knew too well
          Ocean's waves were rough ;
And it needed none to tell
That all Europe banded so
For his *final* overthrow.

Very soon that rock became
Crowned with vast, undying fame ;

The whole·world was turned to see
Napoleon in captivity.
Monarch was he still, as grand
As when, hearing his command,
Armies rose, and kingdoms fell
As beneath some fatal spell.
But slowly passed his life away,
    Filled with utter dreariness ;
Heavy grew each sultry day,
    Bringing with it naught to bless
    Save the constant tenderness
Of the friends who sought to be
Comfort in his misery.
Death was gaining in the race ;
    All the signs were visible
In the exiled monarch's face —
    Torture did its mission well.
Five long, dreary, painful years
    Had on lagging wings gone by,
Since, engulfed in blood and tears,
    France had met his anxious eye.
Five long years, in restless pain,
    He had borne captivity ;
In the sixth year Azrael came
And announced his liberty.

DEATH OF NAPOLEON.

The night was wild, and the winds were high,
And black clouds scud o'er a blacker sky ;
And a flood of beating, blinding rain
Swept o'er that rock in a hurricane.

Loud bellowed 'the thunder, crash upon crash,
And the night was lit with the lightning's flash;
And the waves on the rocky shore broke high,
With a mournful dash and a plaintive cry,
Wildly and weirdly, and fit to be
The last sad wail of a soul set free.
Unknowing it all, the Emperor lay
Dreaming of things that were far away;
His lofty brow was as lofty still
As when empires bent beneath his will;
Nature had stamped on that forehead high
The gift of her own grand royalty.
'Round the dying man were grouped a few.
To watch as he slowly struggled through
The " river of death," — the winds outside
A requiem fit for the scene inside.
But he did not hear the storm without,
He heard but the wilder battle shout;
Again he charged on the flying foe
O'er the trampled plains of Marengo;
Again he shouted in accents clear,
" Forward! retreat not when I am here!"
And then he looks on a sweeter scene
And tenderly murmurs of Josephine.

At last, through the gloom of that awful night
The soul of Napoleon took its flight;
A fitting close to his life's wild scene
Were his last words, " Army! France! Josephine!"
Marble, majestic, his friends scarce knew
The stormy journey at last was through.

They shrouded him then, as, dressed in life,
He had rode through the battle's fiercest strife :
O, royal dress ! O, mournful fate ! —
O, sequel grand for a life so great!

. . . .

They buried him there on that dreary rock,
And Tyranny rose with a terrible shock ;
For when he sank to his lonesome grave
There were sobs from the hearts of millions brave ;
Kingdoms were shaken with unfeigned woe —
He was Emperor still, though he slept so low ;
Emperor yet, though a nameless stone
Covered the exile from land and throne ;
And Helena was spoke as a sacred name —
The burial place of a man of fame.

. . . .

England now had done her worst ;
She who will forever boast
Of her laws, her truth, her right,
Had disgraced her sceptre quite,
And had made her name accursed.
Never will her proud sons hear
St. Helena without shame ;
Never can she hope to clear
From her honor that foul stain.
Yet she could not crush him down
Though she robbed him of his crown,
For his fame is spreading wide,
And his name is glorified.

Nineteen years the hero slept
On that rock by ocean swept.

Nineteen years ! and then the land
Rose with exultation grand,
And united, all as one,
Cried aloud, " Give us Napoleon ! "
Filled with mingled joy and grief
Welcomed they their slumbering chief.
Cannon thundered as 'twas wont
When he dashed to battle's front ;
Music wailed, and banners swung
Over flowers by fair hands flung ;
Trembled all the air with song,
As the cortege moved along ;
Lofty arches, statues proud,
'Long the pathway rose and bowed.
Bayonets were flashing bright,
As when ere some coming fight,
He had scanned, with practiced eye,
Their unspotted brilliancy ;
Veteran eyes were dim with tears,
And the thunderous, thrilling cheers
Told full well the nation's gladness,
Mingled with peculiar sadness.
In this royal state, and drawn
By superbest coursers, on
Passed the last remains of him
Who was deaf to all this din.
Could his spirit, looking down,
Glory in this great renown ?
Saw he not his welcome home
To the army, people, throne ?
Ah ! I know not ; I can tell

Only of these mortal scenes ;
Something, which perhaps is well,
  'Tween the two worlds intervenes.
Only can I know, at last
  Proudly does his dust repose
Where his glorious life was passed —
Now secure from all his foes.
Only can I know yon shaft [1]
  Rising upward, rears his form,
Lifelike, clear, and towering high,
  Kissed by sun, unshook by storm,
And his fame, o'er every sea,
Is increasing steadily.
Rest, Napoleon ! grandest man
In the great Almighty's plan.
Few now wonder where thou'st trod,
Thou art thought almost a god.[2]

[1] The column of the Grand Army in the Place Vendôme
which has since been torn down by the Commune.
[2] " Napoleon was the greatest of the creations of God."
                                    LAMARTINE.

MISCELLANEOUS POEMS.

————◆————

"O, PLEASANT it is for the heart
  To gather up itself apart
  To think its own thoughts, and to be
  Free as none ever yet were free,
  When, prisoners to their gilded thrall,
  Vain crowd meets crowd in lighted hall,
  With frozen feelings, tutored eye,
  And a smile which is itself a lie."
                    From the " Lost Pleiad."

      " The fiery-footed barb
That pounds the pampas, and the lily bells
That hang above the brooks, present the world
With no apology for being there,
And no attempt to justify themselves
In uselessness. It is enough for God
That they are beautiful and hold his thought
In fine embodiment ; and it shall be
Enough for me that, in this book of mine,
I have created somewhat that is strong
And beautiful, which, if it profit — well !
If not, 'tis no less strong and beautiful,
And holds its being by no feebler right."
                    From " Kathrina."

MISCELLANEOUS POEMS.

MY LIFE–BATTLE.

SHALL I yield up the battle of life in despair,
   That the mountainous billows of sorrow surge
      o'er me?
Shall I close my heart's portals to everything fair,
   And live in the gloom that alone seems before
      me?

Shall I yield to the weight of the burden I bear?
   Shall I say to the world, I am weak, I am
      weary?
Shall the silver creep into the brown of my hair
   Because my sad life has grown utterly dreary?

Shall I fold my hands idly, nor toil any more?
   Are there not some others who struggle with
      sorrow?
Though the path may be rough, and thy feet may
      be sore,
   May not there be glory and gladness to-morrow?

MY LAND IDEAL.

I STOOD in the city, musing,
   In the whirr of the busy street;
My eyes were on pictures gazing,
   My thoughts were on you, my sweet.
Aye, riotous tides of feeling
   Ran over the barrier, pride;
All things grew dim in my vision,
   E'en they who stood by my side.

Far away to a glorious region,
   From the traffic of soul and sense,
I had fled, with a grievous longing
   For something like recompense:
Some subtle, sweet thrill of gladness,
   Some passionate clasp of hands,
Which should gather me up and place me
   The foremost in all the lands.

I longed for the tender tokens
   Of a heart which was all my own;
Mine blossomed like roses in summer, —
   Yet I stood in the streets alone.
Fair landscapes rose up before me
   Through the gleam of a silver mist,
With lilies that paled and quivered
   By the breath of the morning kissed.

O, the dreamy delight that thrilled me
In the hum of the busy street!
I was roaming away in vision,
With my hand in yours, my sweet.
You will stay in my land ideal,
You will dream with me dreams, and see
How the rosy tints of affection
Will color my destiny.

A LOVER'S RHAPSODIES.

I KNOW a little girl, she is very fair to see ;
There may be others fairer, but she seemeth best
    to me ;
For her dainty little feet, as they trip along my way,
Have a grace that does not vanish in the common
    work of day.

Her brow is white enough, and her bonny shining
    hair
Is parted smooth above it with just enough of care ;
Some poets call it golden ; it may or may not be,
But I'm sure 'tis very pretty when she dresses it
    for me.

This little girl has eyes of the deepest, darkest blue,
But they sometimes speak a language that cannot
    be known to you ;
Perhaps there may be others that employ this
    cunning art,
But these alone have power to search deep into
    my heart.

My little girl has teeth of the dazzling hue of snow,
And enough of healthful knowledge to keep them
    always so ;

Her cheeks are beds of roses where dimples hide
    and seek,
And blushes glimmer faintly when I dare my love
    to speak.

My little girl has hands that are quite as soft and
    white
As the drifts of snow that gather at my door-stone
    in the night;
But when I clasp the fingers, as they flutter to
    and fro,
I find them warm and human, which cannot be
    said of snow.

My little girl is pure as the lily when it blows,
And the dallying winds deal gently with her bo-
    som's spotless snows;
But they cannot be more gentle than the arms
    that have embraced
With a lover's tender passion the ungirded little
    waist.

My little girl has lips that are ruby red, and sweet:
When I kiss them in the twilight my bliss is quite
    complete ;
For then this little fairy, who has seemed to need
    no rest,
Seeks the shelter of my arms and nestles on my
    breast.

LOVE VERSUS GOLD.

UNBIND the braids of my hair, sweet friend,
For my heart is sick and sore ;
And I fain would take from my weary form
The things that to-night I wore.
For I cannot, sweet friend, I cannot bear
The weight of these flowers upon my hair ;
For their rich perfume but brings to me
Strange thoughts of the night's wild revelry.

And undo this silken dress, sweet friend,
I hate each gleaming fold ;
For I cannot bear to think, sweet friend,
That to-night I bowed to gold.
That the flowers which shone in my hair to-night
Have brought to my soul a withering blight ;
The hand which has lain in a dearer one
Was given to-night — and my soul 's undone.

Did you hear the music sob, sweet friend,
And the sound upon the floor?
The light of the lamps was a terrible thing —
And my age is scarce a score.
There were regal heads, there were brows of snow,
There were lips that would rival the ruby's glow ;

And the lips of one, with a regal head,
As he bowed to me in the past, had said:

"Come out where the flowers are damp, dear love,
　With the dew that 's falling now,
And lend for a while your pearly ear,
　And list to my solemn vow.
O, queen of my heart! the glittering light
Of your eyes has made me your slave to-night;"
And, bending his knee, — "I love you so,
O, queen of my soul, do not bid me go!"

My heart stood still as I heard, sweet friend,
　For I knew it could not be;
For wealth was the thing I craved, sweet friend,
　And, ah, he had none for me!
And I told him this while my head drooped low,
And my cheek grew white with my heart's wild
　　woe;
I gave him my heart, but I kept my hand,
And now I'm the saddest in all the land.

I cannot forget his face, sweet friend,
　Though the years should come and go;
And though I am proud and cold, sweet friend,
　I love him, I love him so!
As the music rang through the lighted room
It seemed to me like the knell of doom,
For to-morrow I wed with a man I know
I *never can* love — and I love *him* so.

So loosen my braided hair, sweet friend,
  Perhaps 'twill ease this pain ;
And lay these mocking pearls aside
  For the day that will come again ;
Then darken the room, for I hate the light,
And tell me, O, tell me that I am right !
But none of the careless crowd must know
That I wed for gold, with a heart of woe.

HEREAFTER.

It may be that in the realms of bliss
　We shall be once more united ;
That for the sorrow and doubt of this
　The face of the future is lighted.
It may be that where the angels are,
　And their hymns of joy are chanted,
We shall each be crowned with a glorious star,
　And the prayer of our souls be granted.

I think, sometimes, as we kneel at night,
　With the holy hush around us,
That the darkness and gloom are growing bright,
　And the chain is snapped that bound us.
There are miles of river, and lake, and plain,
　Stretched far and wide between us,
But all the torture, and all the pain,
　Of this parting will not demean us.

For, by and by, when each soul is freed
　From this cumbrous earthly prison,
The thirst will be quenched, and every need
　Will be fed in a field Elysian ;
And the gloom which now o'er our pathway lies
　Will be turned to a gleam of glory,
And up in the beautiful, dark blue skies,
　'Twill be as an old, old story.

So let each work with a brave, strong heart,
  And banish all small repining ;
Though fate has thrown us so far apart
  My soul is your life divining.
There 's another life than the one now ours,
  Which waits for the grand endeavor ;
Upheld through *this* by the unseen powers,
  There, *there* we shall love forever.

MAXIMILIAN.

UNLUCKY scion of nobility!
What stern decree of God has brought thee low,
And laid thy head with other men's? Just God!
How power, magnificence, and pride have bowed
To Mexico's imperial edict.
Eagerly thou didst assume the kingly
Purple, and grasp a usurped sceptre's gold.
Strong hands, stout hearts, a nation's right op-
    posed, —
And lo! with bristling walls of steel the hosts
Of bannered France were met, and blood, rich
    blood,
Flowed o'er the fair green soil in lavish tides.
The cannon which announced thy squadron's
    charge
Seemed but an echo of the roar which had
Convulsed our States. Its sullen music died
At last away, but still the thunders shook
Thy borders, and strife and ruin held high
Carnival. Brave men, on either side, have
Fought with valor scarce e'er equaled. Kings'
    pride,
The strongest pride of old imperial France,
Sent an unlucky prince across the waves
To crown himself with an inglorious

Death, and be, in after time, applauded.
Poor prince ! the cause you dared sustain some-
    time
Will fade in smoke and shadow.   Freedom, then,
Will gild with just as gorgeous rays the skies
Of disunited Mexico, as now
She pours her light throughout our own fair land,
And millions, chanting liberty, will sigh
When Maximilian's name is heard.

"LOVE IN A COTTAGE."

A DEAR little cottage under the trees,
 Cozily nestled, snug and white ;
Roses clambering over the porch,
 A leafy veil 'gainst the yellow light.
Breezes wandering in and out
 Shaking the curtain's snow-white fold ;
Sunshine flickering on the floor,
 Quivering there like a shower of gold.

Snowy cloth on the table spread,
 Supper waiting the absent one,
Loving wife with the nut-brown hair
 Anxiously watching the set of sun.
Tea-kettle singing with louder tone,
 Sunshine slanting the carpet o'er,
Girlish wife with a beaming face
 Going oft to the cottage door.

Click of the gate in the sun's last rays ;
 Wife with a hasty step to meet,
Bounding over the greensward path,
 The weary husband to kindly greet.
A cheering smile, and a fond caress,
 She leads him into their pretty home,

The kiss on his lips, and the waiting meal,
  Proving the words, "I'm glad you've come!"

.   .   .   .

The deepening shadows fall one by one,
  And there they sit clasped hand in hand,
The brave young husband, the fair young wife, —
  A home of love in a far-off land.

VENICE, ITALY. 1866.

"BEAUTIFUL Venice! the bride of the sea!"
Crown of the Italy yet to be!
Lo! we are praising thee over the sea,
     Gloria! Gloria!

We too have breasted the brunt of a war,
Lo! we have lost not a Stripe or a Star!
Venice knows well what the battle was for,
     Gloria! Gloria!

Fling out your banners, O nation new born,
Liberty now is not sitting forlorn, —
Free as the winds on the wings of the morn,
     Gloria! Gloria!

God is upheaving the ages to-day,
Learning the people to work and to pray, —
Splendor gleams out from the dark clouds of gray,
     Gloria! Gloria!

Venice, O Venice! thou city of song!
Under thy fetters thou'st groveled too long,
Beautiful *then*, but now splendidly strong,
     Gloria! Gloria!

Welcome your hero with thunderous cheers,
Load him with flowers begemmed with glad tears,
Trumpet his fame through the swift-coming years,
Garibaldi !

Write down his deeds in letters of flame,
Write down your king's by the side of the same —
Beautiful land with a beautiful name —
Italy ! Italy !

Lo ! we cross hands with you over the sea ;
Sing us, Italia, the songs of the free,
Both kneeling low to a crowned Liberty —
Gloria ! Gloria !

O, ye have crowned her as Victor by name, —
We, as a people, are crowned all the same ;
Both have baptized her in blood and in flame,
Liberty ! Liberty !

Venice, O city of art and of pride,
Wedded to ocean, a glorious bride !
Despots shall tremble as we, side by side,
Breast the bold billows of Tyranny's tide,
Columbia ! Italy !

MEMORY'S HOPE.

I'VE dwelt amid the eastern hills,
   I've seen the sunset's glow,
Like billows of a crimson sea,
   Come trembling to and fro,
I've seen the forest's stalwart pride
   Bend to the tempest's blow,
Or rear majestically aloft
   Enwreathed with ice and snow:
But this was in the sunny past,
   Alas! 'twas long ago.

I've listened to the wandering breeze
   Among the dark green leaves;
I've seen the lake's blue billows roll
   When wild unrest upheaves.
I've watched the lazy flight of hours
   From many a sunny hill;
I've heard the thunder shake the air
   As God's almighty will:
An eastern sky bent o'er me then, —
   Alas! it does not still.

I've seen the circling mountain tops
   Stretch upward to the sky,
And Day, begirt with royalty,
   Set on their heights and die.

I've seen the moonlight, soft and bright,
  Bathe many a towering dome
With lustre all as fair, I ween,
  As that which falls on Rome ;
For, ah ! its tender radiance fell
  Around the scenes of home.

And I have watched the crimson light
  Of day's decaying pride
With oriental grandeur fall
  Across the prairies wide ;
And I have seen the gorgeous flowers
  Which dot those prairies o'er,
As if they might be angels' tracks —
  They having passed before :
That was a dream of early days, —
  I dream it now no more.

I've seen the tempest's awful power,
  Encrowned with wreathing flame,
Stoop low to shuddering earth, till we,
  As instinct, breathe God's name ;
But, O ! 'twas then my restless soul
  Exulted in the strife,
And all its passions, fierce and high,
  Waked into sudden life :
O, western thunder-storms, ye are
  With awful grandeur rife !

And I have seen the sunshine fall,
  Like benediction fond,

On many a scene surpassing fair : —
  'Tis then that the Beyond,
The shadowy, distant, great Unknown
  Seems questioning my soul,
And o'er the harp strings of my life
  A flood of feelings roll,
Yet waking not one strain of bliss
  Within my bitter soul.

O, when I watch the ocean wave
  That laves a foreign shore,
Exulting, I will smile at fate,
  And dream of this no more.
The dark blue skies that arch afar,
  The slumberous winds that stir
In scented groves across the sea
  Shall cheer their worshipper,
And memory then will softly sigh
Above the days that were.

THE KINGDOM OF LOVE.

THE world it may crown me with laurel,
  It may lift up my name to the skies,
But praise which alone I e'er covet
  I shall find in the depths of your eyes.
The roar of the millions applauding
  Could not reach to the deeps of my heart,
And you since the day of my giving,
  Have been of my being a part.

No queen whom the kingdom is crowning
  Ever thrilled with such royal delight,
As I when you clasped me and praised me
  In the flush of the morn's rosy light.
'Twas that which my soul had been craving,
  What I wrought for and hoped for so long,
And the touch of your lips in the twilight
  Itself was the birth of a song.

The rose as it bends to the whisper
  Of the breeze when it sweeps to the sea,
Ne'er flushes with purer emotion
  Than my cheek when I listen to thee.
The lake when it heaves its blue bosom
  To the queen of the night in the skies,
Thrills not in its innermost being
  As I 'neath a glance from your eyes.

The world then may crown me with laurel,
    Or refuse to give ear to my lays,
My world is the heart that I covet,
    And my glory the words of its praise.
I'm queen of a realm of the spirit,
    And the tributes this kingdom shall bring,
With tenderest care · I will treasure
    And lay at the feet of my king.

CHRISTMAS.

MERRILY, merrily trip the feet
Of the dancers in the hall, my sweet,
  Merrily now to the music's tone,
  O, the gathered crowd — *and I alone.*

O, Christmas Eve! with your holy sky,
Do you hear the laugh, or heed the sigh?
  Does the music's mirth accord with thee
  And the Christ that trod old Galilee?

How calm the sky, and how sweet the night!
But there's something in my heart not right,
  For the bounding pulse, the lip of flame,
  Have not been caught from the Saviour's name.

Merrily, merrily through the hall
The feet of the dancers now do fall:
  And I thought to make my heart so gay!
  To drive the sadness and doubt away.

Merrily now! O revelers, there,
Bow with me at a solemn prayer;
  Yea, worship Jesus, the star that rose
  And shone o'er Bethlehem's brilliant snows.

Music and mirth, and a goodly crowd,
A ball-room dress, and a costly shroud!
  The merry laugh, and the music's clang,
  Forgetting the song the Shepherds sang!

O, holy day! what a load of sin
The people, through thee, do welcome in!
  'Tis best for me that my reckless feet
  Are far from the brilliant dance, my sweet.

And yet, ah me! ah, the human heart!
The things of earth of its life are part.
  The lamp's bright glare has a charming spell,
  And I love the music all too well.

Merrily, revelers, dance away!
It matters not where we kneel to pray,
  For God's as near in the halls of men
  As in the cradle at Bethlehem.

REACH ME YOUR HAND, DARLING.

REACH me your hand, darling,
  I am waiting alone
In the gleam of the glory,
  Surrounding the Throne.
The angels above me
  Are smiling to see
How eager and anxious
  I'm looking for thee.

Far up over cloudland,
  Secure from life's ills,
My soul with new rapture
  Exultingly thrills.
So long I have waited
  And watched for the sign
Which tells my glad spirit
  Of coming of thine !

Behold ! I am leaning
  From battlements blue,
My soul filled with longing, —
  A longing for you.
For heaven has but illy
  Repaid me your loss,
And the light and the shadow
  Fall checkered across.

Then reach me your hand, darling,
  And hasten from thence,
This message I give thee
  From Omnipotence :
" Haste thou to the spirits,
  The happy, the blest ;
Though .storm-tossed and weary,
  Thou now shalt have rest."

This, this is the message
  With which I now greet
The soul I have loved thus,
  With loving complete.
Reach me your hand, darling,
  As I wait here alone
In the gleam of the glory
  Surrounding the Throne.

No more shall the terror,
  Of earth and its care,
Have power to disturb thee,
  Nor hope, nor despair.
Secure in the glory
  That circles the blest,
O, reach me your hand, darling,
  And learn all the rest.

A WOMAN'S WANTS.

SOME one to look for with anxious delight,
   Some one to kiss when the twilight is over,
Some one to love in the hush of the night,
   Some one to be both a friend and a lover.

Some one to work for, to plan for, caress;
   Some one to look to in joy and in sorrow;
Some one to ask the Good Father to bless,
   Some one to be with to-day and to-morrow.

Some one to talk about what the day brings,
   Some one to cheer up when fretful and dreary;
Some one to bring home an armful of things,
   Some one to say that the home-nest is cheery.

Some one to *rest* in this dear nook of love,
   Some one to battle when storms have descended;
Some one to be all one's own up above,
   To wait for and welcome when life shall be ended.

WE LOVE BUT ONCE.

" Once only.
Affection precious sweets
May through a thousand common channels give,
And yet the chary heart ecstatic beats,
Once only, while we live !"

ALICE CARY.

NEVER but once will the human heart
  Thrill to the music of love's own strain ;
Never, oh, never, though years shall roll,
  Will the glorious vision come again.

Never but once will the angel bright,
  From the starry regions of heaven above, —
Never but once will he touch the soul
  To the glad emotions that spring from love.

Never but once, though the checkered years
  Bring eyes of azure and eyes of jet, —
Never but once will the bosom thrill
  To a glorious dream it can ne'er forget.

Under the skies of a foreign clime,
  Wandering ever from zone to zone,
Still will the human heart, so strange,
  Return and cling to the loved alone.

Never but once will the angel, Love,
  Stir *life's depths* with his balmy breath ;
Never but once, then, grand and true,
  He will meet and conquer the angel, Death.

A BALLAD.

A GALLANT knight, with gems bedight,
    Went riding along the moor;
A lady gay had passed that way,
    Disliked by all the poor.

But the gallant knight, from clear, sheer spite,
    Followed the lady gay,
Although his care for one more fair
    Went with him night and day.

With speed he rode to a grand abode,
    And knelt at the lady's feet;
But his heart was sore, for no, no more
    Might he dream of a face more sweet.

'Twas a castle grand, in a foreign land,
    Where the gallant knight the lady bore;
Banners of pride swayed far and wide,
    And draped the massy door.

And silver plate, from an old estate,
    Shone bright on the marble board,
And servants proud smiled much, and bowed
    To the knight with the gilded sword.

The new made bride, in her haughty pride,
  Scarce deigned to taste the feast ;
She had wed for gold and her heart was cold,
  Nor thrilled for the knight the least.

As the wine foamed high, and the guests drew nigh,
  A fair form draped in white,
With a pallid face, and a woeful grace,
  Bowed low before the knight.

"Sir Knight ! Sir Knight !" moaned the lips so
      white,
  "You have broken an awful vow ;
Behold ! true steel your heart shall feel,
  And I'll make your knees to bow."

And the guests looked up from each silver cup,
  As the reeking dagger swung
In the maid's small hand, ere the dread command
  Had hardly left her tongue.

But no one stirred, although all heard,
  And the maniac girl went free : —
Some queer folks say, that wed that way
  The devil *will* have the fee.

TO-DAY.

I AM not sad to-day:
  The inner sanctuaries of my soul
Have not been stormed and given away;
  I do not hear the awful roll
  Of muttered thunder, such as stole
From out the heavens when Christ was crucified,
And Jewish spears went through his bleeding side.

I cannot say I am at rest;
  God's universal law does not arrange it so;
Yet no tumultuous feelings thrill my breast
  While gazing out o'er winter's spotless snow;
  It is not that my blood now moves more slow
Than it has moved in gladder days gone by,
When Heaven seemed plain and clear before mine
      eye.

I am not sad to-night,
  Though nations pass before my eyes,
Some raising standards for the right,
  Some raising wrong that surely dies,
  All glorified with songs and cries
Which tell of deeds that color lands with fame,
And give unto a people place and name.

Dissembling France I see,
  With purple hands behind her king,
And leering at the powers that be,
  She lists to hear Italian songsters sing,
  Whose freedom thrills through every lyre's rent
      string,
And to the Old World's waiting nations speaks
In language crimson as the sunset streaks.

I am not sad to-day ;
  For God, the Christ, the King,
I know sits high above this heaving world ;
  And as her warriors fight, and poets sing,
And States are shaken with new flags unfurled,
His hand alone, with grand almighty skill,
Will raise that nation most which most exalts his
      will.

THE COUNT ST. JAMES.

'Twas a lovely day in the month of May,
The hills were green and the birds were gay,
And the graceful fall of the fountains fair,
Flung bewitching music upon the air.   '

The light leaves shook as the murmuring brook
Caught up the tune that the wild birds took ;
But the darkened cheek of the Count St. James
Was dyed with the hue of the summer flames

By his side there sat, with off-flung hat,
Sweet Alice, the rose of Avondat ;
And the blushes flew o'er her pure, fair face,
As he clasped her oft in a wild embrace.

" O, fly with me ! far over the sea,
Where the birds sing love from each bush and tree,
Where the blush that gleams on the Morning's brow
E'en rivals the blush that I gaze on now.

" There 's a trusty crew that await for you
In the bay that is hid by the rocks from view ;
And a bright, rich isle over Ocean's foam, —
And there, sweet love, is our rose-wreathed home."

Quick from her cheek fled the crimson streak,
A language more plain than lips could speak;
And the quivering lips and downcast eyes
Were passionate pictures of Love's replies.

Sweet Alice was fair as the mountain air,
And pure as the breath of a living prayer;
But the Count's fond words had reached her heart,
And passion upheaved with a sudden start.

"I fly with thee? yet wherefore flee,
Since I the Countess St. James shall be?
If you love so well what need of flight?
The isle may be fair but our lives less bright."

In his eyes there lay a fire that day,
But his lips love-words could gently say,
And he knew, by the hue of her changing cheek,
The words that his burning lips might speak.

"To-night we fly, or the sunset sky
Will look on a lasting, a long good-by;
In yonder hall there will come disgrace
To my wife, the Countess, with queenly face.

"What, love! start'st thou? by that snowy brow!
You love me not or would ne'er shrink now,
Because ere I'd seen thy fair, sweet face
I had clasped another in my embrace."

The snowy brow grew like crimson now
At his careless jest of the marriage vow,
But her trusting heart had forever been
So free from guilt that it knew no sin.

Lo! the tempter came, and from lips of flame
Presented vice under virtue's name,
And the thrill that his words in her bosom woke
Had left her weak as had lightning stroke.

.   .   .   .

In a hall of pride there 's a disgraced bride,
But a fawning, worshipping world outside,
For the Countess' brow is proud and high,
And her diamonds' gleam like her flashing eye.

Her heart might break, but she still would make
Them think it was not for his false sake ;
She would hide whatever she felt of woe,
And the tempter and tempted alike might go.

'Twas a brave despair, but the mask we wear
To cover some woe or corroding care,
Oft poisons the blood, and sinks more deep
The pain of the hurt, till we fain would weep.

And the Countess grew (though the outside crew
Could discern no change to their blinded view)
To be but a hollow, though brilliant thing,
Over which her jewels no warmth could fling.

But she sank at last, and the trial past,
Death severed, with quick, relentless grasp,
The chords of the heart that had long been cold,
And the Countess died with her woe untold.

.   .   .   .

In a rose-wreathed bower, at the twilight hour,
When the heart feels most love's bewitching power,
Lay a form like a sculptured marble stone,
With a brow more white which the sun glanced on.

There were signs of woe o'er the cheek of snow,
Where once bright flushes did come and go,
And the long, fair hair o'er her bosom flung
Had tangled the beams of the setting sun.

Like an angel hurled from the upper world,
Where his banner of light the Day King furled,
'Round whom all the glory of heaven still flames,
Lay sweet Alice : — and where was the Count St.
        James ?

In a lighted hall, where fleet feet fall,
He kneels to a lady who smiles on all ;
For her flashing eyes and her jetty hair
Have tired his heart of a face more fair.

And he gave to her, as a worshipper
Gives costliest jewels, and spice, and myrrh,
The love of a heart that till then had known
Not one throb of love — *pure love* alone.

O, he loved at last, for the fiery blast
Of passion had withered away and passed;
And he clasps a hand of bejeweled snow,
And he whispers, "Dear lady, O, must I go?"

In her clear, dark eye gleamed a purpose high,
As her red lips trembled to this reply:
"Go! seek in an isle o'er the broad, blue sea
The life you have ruined and left for me!

" I scorn your vow! ah, 'tis well you bow
To a power you never have felt till now;
Like *hers* you would mingle *my* life with woe —
I hate you, despise you, and bid you go!"

As the heart is shocked when the grating lock
Shuts down on our lives like a wind hurled rock,
So those few harsh words, with resistless might,
Filled the life of St. James with a dungeon's night.

He 'rose, he went; but his form was bent,
As a score of years their weight had lent;
And the pallid hue of his cheek and brow
Proved but too truly strong hearts may bow.

He had loved, and well o'er his bosom fell
The withering blight of an earthly hell;
But he sought, as his lady had bade him seek,
A wasted form and a whitened cheek.

Over wave and foam, with a weary moan,
He sought out the isle he had left to roam ;
His heart was heavy, and wild his brain,
And his soul seemed left to consuming pain.

He reached the shore, and his feet once more
Trod the paths they so oft had trod before ;
And he sought again the once-loved bower
Where song and passion had winged each hour.

The roses fell with a soothing spell,
As if of their mistress they fain would tell ;
He. parted the vines, — but why forsook
All the blood his lips, as his stout form shook ?

A still, white face, in the once loved place,
Bore of life and love not the slightest trace ;
The lips were mute, and the fair hair fell
O'er a silent heart ; — *it had loved too well.*
    . . . .
In other lands soon he clasped fair hands,
'Mong the Alps' white snows, and the desert
        sands ;
But he died, a reckless and wretched thing,
With a curse on his lips for his wandering.

DARLING.

DID you ever call me darling,
  With a flush upon your cheek?
Know you not my heart thrills ever
  To the slightest word you speak?
Do you never guess how pleasant
  Are the moments spent with you?
That this strange, intense affection
  Links my soul with all that 's true?

Yes, you called me darling, one time,
  In a tone so sweet and low
That its music thrills me ever,
  Cheering me where'er I go.
Night was round us, soft and dewy,
  Fragrant with the summer flowers,
And on wings of swiftest fleeing
  Sped the bright, entrancing hours.

Angels hovered in the shadows,
  Whispering holy things to me,
Sounding through my spirit's cloisters
  A bewildering symphony.
Darling! never word of passion,
  But this tender, thrilling one,
Sweet as that which charmed the lovers
  When the world had first begun.

And it charmed me, thrilled me, filled me
  With supremest happiness ;
Not for king, with crown and sceptre,
  Would I give that one caress.
Your hand mine was fondly clasping —
  In its grasp my future lay,
For a love then sprang to being
  Which will never know decay.

ALICE CARY.

THE world has lost a splendor
  From the starry realms of song, —
The voice whose thrilling sweetness
  Has charmed the world so long.
E'en the lowly wildwood daisies,
  As they nod on prairies free,
Will miss the breezy fragrance
  Of her wondrous melody.

In woodland nooks and hollows,
  Where violets shade their blue,
Will Nature shed her tear-drops
  In drops of crystal dew ;
And stars that come out nightly,
  On the firmament o'erhead,
Will shine in softer glory
  O'er the spot where she lies dead.

But when Spring-time brings the flowers,
  Looking upward to the sky,
They will speak with prophet voice
  Of her immortality ;
While beyond the sunset's splendor
  She will list with radiant eyes,
And retune her heavenly lyre
  To the airs of Paradise.

WORLD-WEARY.

If afar from toil and turmoil
  I might rest awhile with thee,
Earth would hold no gladder spirit,
  None more fraught with melody.
Every bird would sing an anthem,
  Every blossom glow with praise,
All that nature strews around me
. Would but wing the gladsome days.

Never would my soul grow weary,
  Resting thus afar with thee,
For one love which fondly shelters
  Is enough to comfort me.
Love would make the roses blossom
  With a dear, delicious red,
Love would change to clearest azure
  Every threatening cloud o'erhead.

O, beloved! amid the toiling,
  When the twilight creeps apace,
How I long to nestle closely
  In a restful, long embrace:
Nestle, knowing that the future
  Holds not days of work and pain,
But the brightness and the triumph
  Of a loss which is our gain.

So, I drift away in dream-land,
  Drift away in dreaming rest;
Nothing more my tried heart craveth
  Save the shelter of your breast.
Pass, O world of work and worry,
  Leave me to my world of love!
Wake me not from this reposing
  'Till I wake in lands above.

TEMPTATION.

'Twas a scene of gorgeous pleasure,
  Incense-laden, crimsoned air,
And the light of lamps gleamed softly
  O'er the proud, the gay, and fair.

Forms there were like sculptured beauty ;
  Eyes whose light outshone the stars ;
Brows of grandness like the angels', —
  But, alas ! an earth-stain mars.

Winning lips with words whose sweetness
  Seemed the chant of angel strain ;
But in all this sweetness mingled
  Earthly passion's restless pain.

And the wine-cup, brightly gleaming,
  Carelessly by fair hands raised,
Lent a most bewitching seeming
  To the hope of future days.

Red lips sang of love and gladness,
  Sipping fast the ruby wine ;
'Mid that festive scene no sadness
  Seemed to touch the brow of Time.

Music trilled her softest measure,
  Bright eyes. flashed with mirth and pride ;
But down, down beneath the pleasure
  Might not awful anguish hide ?

Yes, ah, yes ! from scene so pleasant
  Let us follow some away ;
Look ye now upon the present,
  Then upon a future day.

There stands one ! A man whose genius
  Is in burning words displayed,
And whose eloquence, outbursting,
  Senate House and Halls has swayed.

On his brow, already, laurel
  By the people's hands is flung,
And his power to mould and fashion
  Flaming thought is on each tongue.

See ! he drains the sparkling goblet
  Till its brightness fills his eyes ;
And as one inspired he talketh, —
  But the inspiration dies.

Follow to that princely dwelling
  In the lone hours of the night ;
Little need much more of telling —
  Lo ! so soon has come the blight.

Anxiously the fond wife meets him ;
  That her noble husband ! he
Whom she once so proudly welcomed
  Crowned with wreaths of Poesie !

Yes, his genius is extinguished ;
  Groveling there he seems a beast :
But he came from halls of *prestige*,
  From a most *distingué* feast.

Curses on the world of fashion !
  Curses on these tempting things !
Why *will* men and women tempt us
  To partake of that which stings ?
    .   .   .   .

Once more, reader, from that meeting
  We will trace another life ;
Out amid the hurrying life-tide,
  From a scene with beauty rife.

There she stands ! a royal woman,
  In the pride of womanhood ;
Power and strength look from her features, —
  Mighty power for doing good.

Fashionable ! she sipped the dainty,
  Tempting, rosy, sparkling wine,
Carelessly amid the gathering,
  Losing strength for future time.

Disappointments, sharp and bitter,
  Overtook her by and by ;
She had overleaped the barrier, —
  'Twas no easy thing to die.

So she said : " I like the burning
  Of the wine ; *I'll drown my grief !* "
See you not there 's no returning?
  And her sequel, too, is brief.

Fashion ! wine ! disgrace ! now, dying,
  Trace it to the first rash act ;
Do not trust yourself to tamper
  With the wine — look at the *fact.*

Once again be curses ever
  On the lips that dare to say, —
" Drink ! your strength is equal to it ;
  Drink ! enjoy yourself to-day ! "

Down with wine ! yea, down with fashion !
  Lift the temperance banner high !
Drink the beverage God has ordered, —
  Wine whose worth is purity.

MORNING ON THE MOUNTAINS.

LIST ! the rush of breezy pinions !
  Lo ! the spirits of the air !
Lift your brow ! behold the glory
  Beaming, glowing everywhere !
On the hills the trees are stirring
  With a strange, mysterious voice,
And the gleaming peaks of mountains
  In the morning rays rejoice.

Bare your brow before these tokens
  Of a wiser One than we,
And, amid the glow and silence,
  Bow thee once, most reverently.
Let the mountains, and the sunlight,
  And the glorious hues of morn
Teach that for a life of *purpose*
  Men and women have been born.
Search your heart, and read its secrets
  On the mountains grand and lone,
And, when once again you meet me,
  Bring me thoughts akin my own.

THE DYING GIRL TO HER MOTHER.

KEEP the homestead pleasant, mother,
  As it was in days gone by ;
Childhood's home ! I loved it dearly,
  But, dear mother, I shall die.
I can see the green trees swaying
  In the pleasant summer breeze,
And my heart beats slow and sadly
  As I sit and muse of these.

There are many comforts, mother,
  In our home upon the hill,
But I shall not need them, mother,
  When this aching heart is still.
Keep them for your other daughter
  Who has staid to give you cheer ;
Keep them, though unto the wanderer
  They were always very dear.

You have thought the bright green homestead,
  Our home, mother, far away,
Would be brighter if *our* voices
  Made glad music there some day.
But the voice of her who wanders
  Never more will wake to song,
For the heart, from which springs music,
  Has been sorrowful too long.

I can see each clean room, mother,
  All the flowers I left one day,
All the wood, and all the meadows,
  Where I used alone to stray.
But there are some *other* memories,
  More than these, that stir my heart;
So I cannot see you, mother!
  Thus I think as tear-drops start.

I had hoped to bind my forehead
  With the laurel wreath of fame;
But I fear your little daughter
  Ne'er will earn a lifted name.
I can work no longer, mother,
  I am longing so for rest;
Earth will not deny me always:
  I shall gladly seek her breast.

Do not grieve for me, dear mother,
  Though I see my home no more;
I remember every footpath
  Which was dear to me of yore;
Give your presents to my sister, —
  Of them I shall ne'er have need;
Only don't forget me, mother,
  When these few fond lines you read.

Dear old home! so bright and pleasant,
  Happy hours I've spent in thee!
But I've found, as years roll onward,
  Life is but a troubled sea.

You will not forget me, mother,
    Father, sister, brother, all ;
For my love, and stern ambition,
    I am now beyond recall.

RICHMOND ON THE JAMES.

I.

A SOLDIER boy lay dying on a distant Southern plain,
For the minnie balls had fallen like a thickly fall-
ing rain,
And the boy, his blue eyes glazing, to a comrade
reached his hand,
And bade him tell it softly in his blue-skied
Northern land,
The story that, unwilling, his dying lips now spoke,
For 'twould fall upon his loved ones like a sud-
den thunder-stroke :
" O, tell them not I died in the torture of these
pains,
While our flag was proudly floating over Richmond
on the James."

II.

" Now, brother, comrade, listen to the words I have
to say,
They may save you much of sorrow in some future,
reckless day ;
Though you scarcely may believe it, yet the wreck
which now you see
Came from drinking of the wine when it sparkles
brilliantly ;

'I was wild and careless, comrade, when I came
    away from home,
·And the genial, merry Southrons led me farther
    on to roam ;
'I liked their life of pleasure, — from drink scarce
    one abstains, —
·But this was far at Richmond — at Richmond on
    the James.

III.

" 'Twas a scene of maddest pleasure, for the South-
    ern pride was there, —
One might feel its power and passion in the richly
    laden air ;
I had come to see the Southland, and the war
    had broken forth,
I had written to my mother that she soon would
    see me North ;
I'd been thinking of this, comrade, 'mid the music
    and the whirl,
Together with the image of a fair-haired, loving
    girl ;
But soon I did forget them 'mid the wine and
    music's strains,
And I sold my birthright, comrade, at Richmond
    on the James.

IV.

" You may think it not becoming, in a man of
    mind and pride,
That the sparkle of the wine drowned the thought
    of all beside ;

Yet I sipped the ruby wine 'till my reason fled
    away —
For I joined the Southern army ere the rosy dawn
    of day ;
The wine had made me drunken, and, bereft of
    reason's light,
I joined the bands of traitors, and hastened to the
    fight ;
Yes, I signed my name there, comrade, 'mong many
    other names,
That ill-fated night at Richmond — at Richmond
    on the James.

v.

" I can tell but little more, for my breath is grow-
    ing less ;
How my dear ones' hearts are aching, O, comrade,
    you can guess ;
But I can't forbear to ask you if my place among
    the dead
Resulted not from looking on ' the wine when it was
    red ? '
Had I heeded mother's warning, and the earnest
    words of one
Whose happiness, I fear, is for evermore undone,
I might have now been dying where the fire of
    freedom flames, —
A patriot, and a victor, at Richmond on the James.

vi.

" Tell my story gently, comrade, when you say that
    I'm no more,

And be to *her* a brother, the kindest, I implore ;
But to all the boys, in accents that are loud and
      earnest, tell
If they look upon the wine cup 'tis the first step
      straight to Hell ;
O, I pray you do beseech them ! — but my heart
      is growing cold —
God help you, comrade ; profit by the story I have
      told ! "
Then the blue eyes opened wildly, and the pale
      · lips ceased to move,
And some one's white-browed darling was deaf to
      human love :
One more victim of the wine-cup lay there free
      from mortal pains,
While the starry Flag swayed proudly over Rich-
      mond on the James.

LINES,

WRITTEN AFTER RECEIVING A BOUQUET OF ROSES, WITH THE
MESSAGE THAT IT CONTAINED A KISS.

So you sent a kiss this morning
    In the roses June calls hers ;
Sent it to the most devoted
    Of her beauty's worshippers.
Just *one* kiss ? I failed to find *one*,
    For each rose seemed to enfold
Many kisses, much affection,
    Which I'd not exchange for gold.
All the roses bent them softly
    With the love they told to me,
And I kissed *them* for the *giver*,
    Loving *both* right loyally.

CHRISTMAS BANQUET SONG.

'Tis Christmas night, the skies are bright,
  And brightly glows the hearth ;
From far and near come words of cheer,
  And many a sound of mirth.
Few, few there be this side the sea
  Who now feel less of care,
And none on all this earthly ball
  To-night find life more fair.

The table 's spread, wine rare and red
  Foams in the silver cup,
So now, my boys, to Christmas joys
  We'll drink the contents up.
Sweet eyes to-night beam on us bright,
  And lips of ruby hue
Trill out the song, both loud and long,
  And 'sing for me and you.

In hall, or bower, no gladder hour
  For mortals ever shone,
Song, song, and dance, shall soul entrance
  'Till midnight hours are flown.
The roses blush whene'er a hush
  Falls o'er the lighted throng,

Then merry feet, with footsteps fleet,
  Keep pace with liquid song.

Bright heads are bowed among the crowd
  To list a loving tone,
And brows of snow like sunset glow
  When two stray off alone.
O, fairest night! so glad, so bright!
  List not to lovers' sighs,
Young hearts will beat with rapture sweet
  When reading tell-tale eyes.

O, Viol, wake! the silence break
  With notes of joyousness ;
This night, in sooth, is meant for youth,
  And all that it can bless.
Now down the dance, as in a trance,
  We'll trip the measure through,
And in our grasp soft hands we'll clasp
  With pleasure strange and new.

Glide slowly hours, o'er beds of flowers,
  We fain would have you stay ;
Not every heart will dread to part
  With this year's Christmas day.
Come now, again, a louder strain
  From viol and from horn !
With melting glance, and song, and dance,
  We'll usher in the morn.

LIFE'S DARKNESS.

Work on, work on! and a bitter jest
The life which we live becomes, at best;
Who cares for the light of a future day,
If one must forever work and pray?

Work on, work on! as the hours drag by,
And pale lips murmur, would I could die!
Would the busy world, with careless breath,
Stop for one moment above your death?

Why long to die? says the workman bold,
In eager chase for the shining gold;
The world is wide, it is broad and fair,
Why yield your soul to the fiend despair?

Why yield, ye ask? O, ye hearts of stone,
Who cares to live, just *to live* alone?
Who cares for the glare of the yellow gold,
If the hearts that we love are bought and sold?

For what do we climb to the heights of fame,
And work for an everlasting name?
Is it not that the hearts we love the best
Shall thrill with pride as they call us blest?

Work on, work on! when the heart is sick,
And the darkness gathers fast and thick!
And none to censure, and none to praise,
And those we love gone separate ways.

Of what avail is the gaping crowd,
Though the praise they give be long and loud?
Who cares for a future so far ahead?
O, were it not better if one were dead?

Jog on, great world, in your wild, mad strife,
The One who has *given* must *take back* life:
Yet, bitter heart, there's *one* bliss in store, —
'Tis a *shining crown* on the *farther* shore.

MAY, 1864.

WITH the fragrance of the violets
   Comes a lofty, clanging sound,
Though the May breeze rustles over
   The thickly dead-strewn ground
Where our squadrons met in conflict,
   And disputed with the foe
Each inch of grass and daisies,
   Till the soil was red below.

But our Northern violets' fragrance
   Is mingled with a tone
Which tells our brave have perished,
   And a *victory* has been won.
That the Wrong went down so quickly,
   That the Right went up with will;
While the cannon's glad notes ringing
   Give an echo to each hill.

From the Northern soil the violets
   Look with their eyes of blue;
From the Southern soil dead faces
   Uplook for me and you;
For the Right has been triumphant,
   And the Wrong must fall below —
And the South has dead to bury
   While our Northern violets blow.

COSETTE TO MARIUS.

THE tempest was lashing with terror
   The back of a Night in the past,
And the winds, like the voices of demons,
   Were rising up savage and fast,
And the passionate blood of my being
   Grew hot with the fever of youth,
While my spirit, unclad and unshaken,
   Ascended the stairway of Truth.

Then I bowed to the hand that fell on me,
   That fell tenderly down on my head,
And my bosom was throbbing and thrilling
   To the tender, sweet words you had said.
As that hand, in its restless estraying,
   Caressed me with pulses so warm,
All the hidden, fond thrills of my nature
   Awoke in tumultuous storm.

My spirit leaned forth from my features,
   And fearlessly looked from my eyes,
While your passionate mouth drew the kisses
   From my lips in burning replies.
You remember the elements clashing,
   The sheet of the bright wreathing flame,
But do you, my darling, remember
   The tears that I could not restrain?

Then your long, long bewildering glances
  Led my soul. forth to faint and to swoon,
As the Morning lies down with reluctance
  In the tropic embrace of the Noon.
I knew not, I cared not if whirlwinds
  Then frowned from the black stormy sky,
For my soul, like a Queen robed in purple,
  Had dared the whole world to pass ·by ;
For the floods of my sensuous being
  Rose in tides, like the tides of the sea,
And now, though we long have been parted,
  They threaten to overwhelm me.

THE VOICE OF THE WOOD.

I 've wandered in the wood to-day,
  My soul with music stirred ;
It seemed your spirit bent to hear
  Each lightly whispered word.
The leaves lay thick upon the earth,
  The sunlight's luscious hue
Came flickering down upon my head
  As when I sat by you.

O, these are royal, golden days,
  .And waken in my soul
A thousand thoughts I cannot tell,
  Which o'er my bosom roll.
The far-off whisper of the winds
  Among the dropping leaves
Seems to my ear a spirit-voice,
  Which gladdens, and yet grieves.

Yet notwithstanding Nature's calm,
  So fair, so soft, so still,
Tempestuous thoughts within my soul
  My being's pulses thrill.
The beckoning years stand off afar
  Through Autumn's hazy gold,
And bid me walk the heights ahead
  Although my heart be cold.

And then the Past, with noiseless feet,
　Comes to me warningly,
And tells me of the spirit's dearth
　Across Ambition's sea.

With solemn sacredness the leaves
　Are falling, one by one ;
Above, the grand blue sky is arched,
　Around me beams the sun ;
And, through the mysteries of air,
　That magic voice again
Wakes in my being's depths what I
　Can scarce call bliss or pain.

Come near, O, disembodied voice !
　And touch the chords of song ;
The tones that erst were wont to gush
　Have buried been too long.
Wake up again within my soul
　Their passion, power, and pride ;
And let me dream my spirit's force
　Once more walks far and wide.

O, wondrous, mystic human life !
　O, mighty power of mind !
The thrills which through all nature sweep
　My soul has half defined.
The bending sky is God's own book,
　His smile the yellow air ;
The murmur is a voice of love
　Which thrills me everywhere.

11

LINCOLN'S DEATH.

Toll, toll the bell from the highest towers of earth!
Toll, toll the bell to the farthest ends of earth!
Lost, lost, aye, lost to the world for evermore,
He who would have steered the Ship of State to
    shore
Through the awful peril of this awful time —
Meekly great, and unpresumingly sublime.
O, patriot friend! O, royal one of earth!
   Tried in the furnace of a direful wrath!
Thou now art gone, aye, gone to heaven from
    earth,
   With none to follow in thy princely path.
The nation rocks, may founder without thee;
Listen! the tyrants laugh across the sea.
O, man of might! O, man of matchless worth!
For him toll all the grandest bells of earth!
A nation mourns! each heart has throbs of pain!
How lightning quick the awful news came on
And scattered grief o'er all this wide domain,
And made flushed faces, O, so pale and wan!
Our noble President, who was to be
   Our guardian, friend, protector, all, lies dead;
Not, not disease, but murderers' hands have made
   Our grand, gigantic nation lose its head,
To drift about upon an unknown sea.

Yet this the question — should we be dismayed?
  The Lord Almighty guards his people yet;
And He has called to higher station him
  Whose latter life, so rough, had never fret
Or furious passion in it. Calm, and high, and true,
He did, with earnest will, the work he had to do,
And millions blessed him; — though, albeit, *some*
  Denied the good he did; for never one uprose
To carping foes so leniently dumb
    As he who slumbers now in great and grand
      repose; —
The kind heart still, the exerted brain at rest —
A mighty sun gone out upon the fiery west;
Set amid cannon-thunder, pealing victory,
And flags and banners swaying all triumphantly
  Above the traitors' ransacked, reclaimed soil.
A fitting time, methinks, for that great soul,
  A nation's centre — from its mighty toil
To cease, and 'mid red blood and glory mount
    above: —
One human life full-crowned with deeds of love.

      .   .   .   .

The nation rights! I see her, through the gloom,
  Steer safely o'er the shoals which are before;
The pole-star to her course — *our Lincoln's tomb;* —
  He who can labor with us, nevermore.
Our sun is set, but light enough remains
  To guide our Ship of State to cálmest peace;
That light will linger till the bloody stains
  Of treason fade. So, royally release
The spirit of our God-lent Champion. Toll! toll!

With dirge of bells, and cannon's thunderous roll!
Lower the flags of the nation, lower, and low!
Muffle the drums of the nation! all we know
Wringeth the nation's heart! Roll, roll! Toll, toll,
      toll!
For the Lord God has called for a kingly soul.

HAPPINESS.

O, HAPPINESS! thou art my theme,
And I will tell like what you seem.
To most you seem a solid gem
   Which every hand can grasp with ease,
A light and graceful diadem
   Which all can don whene'er they please.
To me you seem a pleasant day,
A path with flowers strewn all the way;
A clasping hand, and love-low voice,
And two hearts beating to rejoice;
Two kneeling down, in solemn trust,
To Him who made them from the dust;
A firm reliance on the One
Who rules afar, beyond the sun,
And, gliding on in peace and calm,
Each moment bathed in heavenly balm; —
Yes, this, to me, seems happiness,
That which humanity would bless.

O, Happiness! now what thou art,
I'll quickly tell with heavy heart;
A magic word which thrills the soul
Till passion's fiercest billows roll;
A dainty phantom, flimsy, light,
Which lures like will-o-wisp at night;

The fatal mirage, traveller-curst,
A dancing bubble, quickly burst ;
A brilliant star, *too high to grasp ;*
A strain of music, quickly past ;
A *nothing* to the longing touch ;
A something that we chase too much ;
Alas ! thou art a silly name,
Ascribed alike to love and fame.
A thing we seek, which, soon as found,
Sinks from our sight into the ground,
And leaves a *shadow,* wondrous less,
And this, by *name,* is Happiness.

THE KNIGHT AND THE MAID.

OVER the waves, on the Old World's shore,
A castle there stood, in days of yore;
Massy, and gloomy, and dark with age,
The home of a knight and youthful page.

A forest behind held flocks of deer,
Before, on the beach, the waves broke clear;
And the sturdy oaks, which graced the lawn,
Sheltered the bounding, beautiful fawn.

And all was grand in that stately home,
Yet the knight prepared himself to roam;
He buckled on sword and massy shield,
And sped away to a battle-field.

O, why did he leave his halls of pride,
His shaven plains and his woodlands wide;
And, above them all, a fair, sweet life,
For war's harsh din, and a scene of strife?

Ah! his was a soul of noblest kind,
Within were valor and truth enshrined;
His native land of her sons had need,
And he proved his rank by royal deed.

The field was red, and the foe was great, —
He kissed a maid by an ivy gate,
Then urged his courser in speed away,
And sought the front of the awful fray.

With breastplate on, and his visor down,
He battled to save his King and crown;
And dealt, with the strength of mighty will,
His blows, till his haughty foes were still.

The King was saved, and the land was free,
Secured by his subjects' bravery;
But the castle's lord, the maiden's love,
Was slumbering low with the sods above.

And down to the gate the maiden goes,
Her black hair wreathed with a wild white rose;
And the castle stands as then of yore,
But the high-souled knight comes never more.

He has a place on the roll of fame,
And his deeds rank high with honor's name;
But the ages come, the ages go, —
And naught says fame of the maiden's woe.

THE LOVER'S MEETING.

I MET her in the streets one day,
 She threw a kiss so sweet to me
That all the air between us thrilled
 And trembled with strange ecstasy.
I saw the dear cheek, purely pale,
 · Glow with a pink so dainty, fine,
That angels must have envied me
 The thoughts which filled this heart of mine.

The passing glance she gave to me
 Was warmest welcome, glad surprise,
And all the loves and graces beamed
 From the dear heaven of her blue eyes;
Some days of absence there had been,
 But now this meeting, sudden, sweet,
Had bridged the emptiness of life
 And brimmed its cup with wine complete.

May the dear hand whose whiteness gave
 That one sweet token of her love,
Cull roses thornless here below,
 And lilies where we meet above;
And when I walk the pass of death,
 If she be crossed to welcome me,
The same dear hand which flung that kiss
 Shall crown my immortality.

APOSTROPHE TO MY LYRE.

Awake, my lyre! in breathings deep and strong,
And burst the fetters which have bound thee long;
Too long in silence have thy numbers slept —
She who awakes them has nor joyed nor wept.
In dumb composure has my soul been bound,
And thus thy strings have quivered to no sound;
But now, from out the tempest tossed within,
Wake up the notes that in the past have been;
Rouse feeling from this dull, chaotic sleep,
And if it be not gay, then let me weep.
No more, my lyre, let silence rust thy strings,
Though every note in saddest music rings.
All Nature now is hushed to wondrous calm,
And this, at least, should bring the spirit balm.
From the dun gray of the horizon sky
Naught meets the wandering, weary, restless eye,
Save stooping hills, and curling wreaths of smoke;
The landscape seems a blessing to invoke.
Some loftier scene, some range of rugged land,
Formed into mountains stretching upward, grand;
Crude, shapeless rocks, with torrents foaming o'er,
Would be in keeping with my feelings more.
The thunder's crash, the lightning's fiery smile,
Would for a time my soul's uproar beguile.

O, human hearts are wondrous mystic things,
And give a thousand tones from thousand strings ;
By little shaken, scarcely jarred by all,
Upraised with naught, and yet with naught to fall ;
Made to search out the mysteries of life,
And yet to be with mystic feelings rife, —
Yet cease, my lyre ! thy notes are wailing low
When in tumultuous music they should flow.
At once breathe out, in one majestic strain,
The feelings pent within, and ne'er again
Seek to revive the tones which once were free,
When soul felt more, or less, tranquillity ;
With one strong note break every quivering string,
And die, as heroes die, in triumphing.

THE BREAKING UP.

I HAVE often heard of the breaking up
  Of the Northern ice and snow ;
Of the torrents which foam and sweep along
  And deluge the world below.
I have heard how the thunder crash comes in
  'Mid the roar of maddened waves
Which carry whole villages down, right down,
  To their scattered, nameless graves.

I have heard how the avalanche comes down
  On the Switzer's home below, —
And likened it to the terrible sweep
  Of some awful, crushing woe :
The breaking up of the ice in Spring,
  To the breaking up of rest,
And the torrents, which rock the river's bed,
  To the sobs which shake the breast.

Ah, me ! when the terrible cry comes in,
  We long for an arm to stay ;
Some hand which will guide o'er the darkened
    path,
  Some one who will point the way.
There is One *above*, — there are none below,
  Of all who are dear to thee,
Who can guide the bark, who can 'save the soul
  That is drifting out at sea.

STORMS.

'Twas a night when the demons seemed loosened,
  For the stars they had gone under cover,
And I lay down weary and weakened
  And thought of a recreant lover.

I had oft read, in olden romances,
  Of the lovers who sang to each other
With a tenderness tearfully thrilling,
  More sweet than a child's for its mother.

Then the heavens grew blacker and blacker,
  And the tempest grew bolder and bolder,   ·
And I prayed for the curly black head
  That had bent till it lay on my shoulder.

For the eyes that were brimful of loving,
  And the brow which the black hair fell over,
And the red lips which quivered at parting, —
  All belonged to my recreant lover.

One day, in the years of my childhood,
  I was maddened with visions of Beauty,
And the love which then sprung into being
  Has forever kept conflict with Duty.

This face I had looked on but rarely,
　　But at last it rose clear on my vision,
And the hair, and the eyes, and the forehead,
　　Were no longer a dream of Elysian.,

But the white hand that oft has caressed me,
　　And the head that has lain on my shoulder,
O God! they are far in the darkness,
　　And the tempest grows bolder and bolder.

May the angels who bend o'er our pathways
　　Be more tender with him than a mother,
And return, when the storm-clouds are rifted,
　　To my bosom this recreant lover.

"KEEP YOUR EYE ON THAT FLAG."

Keep your eye on that Flag! 'tis a beacon of light
    To the millions over the sea,
Who so eagerly look through Oppressions' dark
    night
    To the land of the great and free ;
And, rejoicing, they list to our cannon's fierce roar,
    Which rolls from the Lakes to the main,
While we shout, 'till it reaches that far distant shore :
    Your despots are frowning in vain !

Keep your eye on that Flag! 'tis the rallying sign
    Of the legions this side the waves ;
Its hues, born in heaven, have a meaning divine,
    Which wars with the title of slaves ;
From the tramp of our armies with sinews of steel,
    And our fleets of measureless length,
Lo! the hordes of the traitor and despot now reel,
    Surprised at our terrible strength.

Keep your eye on that Flag! 'tis the emblem of
    Right,
    The hope of the ages to be :
O, how proudly it waves o'er the charge in the
    fight,
    And follows the foe as they flee.

Keep your eye on that Flag! for it heroes have died,
    Who sleep 'neath their green native sod —
Come, ye living! march on in their pathway of pride,
    And fight in this battle for God.

TO A FRIEND.

By every hope my life hath e'er been weaving,
  By all the future holds in store for me,
By every heartless method of deceiving,
  By all we trust our lives are yet to be, —
            I'll not forget thee.

When solemn prayer, upon the soft air breathing,
  Wakes every holy impulse of the soul,
When friends my brow with garlands bright are
      wreathing,
  Or sorrow's tempests fiercely o'er me roll, —
            I'll not forget thee.

And when in chains bright Sleep has softly bound me
  And dreams of friends flit through my resting
      mind,
And guardian angels hover close around me,
  To bring me thoughts of one forever kind, —
            I'll not forget thee.

And O, should some, their truth to me repenting,
  Take back from me the treasure of their love,
And some dark angel stand a cup presenting
  To drown my faith in Him who rules above, —
            I'll not forget thee.

12

Should cruel Fate keep us forever parted,
  Till life's bright lamp is burning dim and low,
And each shall think of each as one departed,
  To clasp the hand of love no more below, —
      I'll *ne'er* forget thee.

FINALE.

GHOSTLY winds on the moor to-night, ghostly winds
    on the moor,
And I hear the click of the moving gate, but no
    foot at the door;
    There are storms at sea, ah me! ah me!
The storms on the sea blow wrecks, blow wrecks
    ashore,
    And none can tell from whence they be.

The hours step soft as they pass along, they are
    velvet-shod, I guess,
And the cold, fair months are gliding by in a brill-
    iant, icy dress;
But winds, and seas, and months, ah me!
Are ghostly cold by the warmth of a lost caress!
And, giddy and gay, 'tis few can pray, and, pray-
    ing, sorrow less.
I sit in the shadow of Egypt's Sphinx, I sit in the
    shade, to-night,
The awful glare of the solemn stars is wrapping me
    'round with light,
And out from the depths of the desert's gloom,
But *not* from the portals of the tomb,
A beautiful face has come once more, a beautiful
    face to me,

And the solemn stars, and the awful Sphinx, and
    even the dreary sea,
In the years to come will be glorified, perchance
    continually.

Ghostly winds on the moor to-night, a wail for the
    royal past,
Lips which were red as rubies, and a love that
    might not last,
For under the sands, and under the waves, there's
    many a fair form lost,
  And the terrible sea with its tides, ah me!
Without a ship can never be crossed, can never be
    crossed.
  Tropic seas have a golden glow, a glow that is
    grand to see,
But terrible clouds come up sometimes, and winds
    rage furiously,
And the desert sands without a guide, the desert
    sands, ah me!
Can never be crossed, and the loved is lost,
And the winds are wailing this out to the sea.

Hope is a dove, the poets say, Hope is a spotless
    dove ;
But this is better, by far, to say, than that the bird
    is Love.
We all commune with the winds and waves, and
    thrill at the tempest's roar,
But a bird, and a dove, we take to our hearts and
    cherish evermore.

But night and morn, and a beautiful face, and all
 the things that be,
Will be lost, I know, except the soul, which will
 live immortally.

Ghostly winds on the moor to-night, oh, winds, ye
 will surely die,
And the stars, those terrible, solemn things, will fall
 from the shaking sky,
And God from earth's remotest pole
Shall gather *together* every soul,
And there shall be not any more sea,
But everywhere awful Immensity.

MY BEAUTIFUL PAST.

How the sunlight gilds the river
   With the rising rays of morn!
And a thousand fond emotions
   In my bosom's depths are born.
Memory, with her wand of magic,
   Brings to me the Summer gone,
.With the rush of Lehigh river
   Sparkling in the rosy dawn.

Once again I hear the murmur
   Of the winds among the pines ;
Once again I see the sunlight
   Glimmer through the creeping vines ;
Comes the perfume of the roses
   That I wore amid my hair,
When, with anxious expectation,
   I was looking for you there.

O, strange memory ! thus recalling
   Love and trust that since have died !
O, weak heart! whose tears well over
   Spite the iron mask of pride !
Rushes still that fair, free river,
   And the sunlight gilds its waves,
Though both Hope and Love are sleeping
   In the gloom of new-made graves.

Still the roses bud and blossom
That I. wore amid my hair ;
But the lips that then caressed me
Never more will make life fair.

Never will the Summer's beauty,
Or the Winter's frost and snow,
Bring to life the tender dreaming
That was ours not long ago.
Gleam of stars and bloom of roses
Are to me not what they were,
From the *Past* alone I gather
All life's frankincense and myrrh.

"THE OLD, OLD STORY."

SIT down in the twilight, dear friend of mine,
  And list to the story I have to tell;
Though it wrings my heart, yet it shall be thine,
  Since I know you have loved me long and well.
Have you forgot where the old Church stood,
  And the chime of its bells in the morning air?
Ah! *have* you forgotten — *I* never could —
  A girl's sweet face which I once saw there?

'Twas a Sabbath morning so bright and clear
  That the birds sang psalms in the leafy trees;
But a face at the door, as I drew near,
  Seemed fairer than any, or all of these.
I never could tell, for the life of me,
  How I entered the Church and sat me down;
Though I heard the sermon I could but see
  This beautiful girl in her humble gown.

And into my being there stole, that day,
  A love that I never can erase;
I know not how God, in his loving care,
  E'er granted me sight of that sweet young face;
For I won the love of that winsome girl,
  Ah, I won her heart, Tom, but just to break;
When I think of it now my brain will whirl, —
  I think of her now asleep or awake.

Long years have passed since the day we met,
  Long years since the night we said good-by ;
But each day is filled with a wild regret,
  And I pray each night, Tom, that I may die.
O, Tom, she loved me ; you cannot know
  How the sweet lips quivered beneath my kiss,
Nor how she told me if I should go
  The earth held, for her, not a hope of bliss.

And can you believe, O Tom, my friend,
  That I vowed I loved her o'er and o'er?
But it came, at last, to a terrible end,
  And I never saw her sweet face more.
I left her, Tom, with a careless jest
  That I might not see her again for years ;
Then, wild with fear, she fell on my breast,
  And plead for my love through her scalding tears ;

I called her "a child ;" I was harsh and cold,
  And I left and was gone for many a day ;
I thought to try her — I wish 'twere told l —
  O Tom, my friend, can you kneel and pray? —
I went at last, but I found her not;
  I found in her stead a marble form ;
And Tom, O Tom ! I shall ne'er forget
  The chill of the lips that were once so warm.

MOONLIGHT FANCIES.

THE moonlight falls in a misty flood
  Adown on my chamber roof,
And a thousand thoughts in my busy brain
  Soon are woven into woof.
I think I stand on Italia's shore,
  And muse as the moonbeams fall
On the glassy sea, and the ivy fanes,
  And many a ruined wall.

It kisses the brow of a fair young bride,
  And sleeps in her sweet dark eyes,
And haloes the spot where the two kneel down,
  Like a gleam from Paradise.
Then I think I see it pouring free
  Down the classic mountain's side,
And it falls in a golden flood on fields
  Where the heroes of earth have died.

Again I stand amid its light
  As it falls on the busy street
Of the city of wit and fickleness,
  Where fashion holds reign complete.
In sunny France, where the vineyards are,
  And the people of dance and song,

And it pours o'er the Bastile a solemn sheen,
  As in fancy' I move along.   ,

It gleams on an old chateau,
  Through its windows, ivy-grown,
Weirdly bright is the moonbeams' light,
  As a dream that is overthrown.
O! it rests on a marble brow,
  On a cheek that is icy cold ;
On the prostrate form of a maiden fair
  Who has sold her life for gold.

Then over the Alps, and far away,
  Where it shines on their peaks of snow,
Gazing, and dreaming, and musing still,
  On fancy's wild wing I go.
It looks in a Switzer's home,
  And rests on the bright young cheek
Of a youth with waving locks flung back,
  And a red lip fixed to speak ;
And his tones are clear and sweet
  As his own free mountain air,
And his proud young face is full of grace,
  Of everything bright and fair.

Away I go where the moonlight sleeps
  On Hungary's sacred soil,
And I see it kiss, with its silver lips,
  A man's brown face of toil.
It rests on the Austrian sabre's blade
  In a soldier's stalwart hand,

And it gleams on Vienna's towering spires
  , As they shadow the verdant land.
And down by a battlement
  It creeps 'mong the cannon balls,
Then speeds away to a pleasant home,
  Where, soft as a prayer, it falls.

Far off in a Turkish harem
  It peeps from the blue, bright skies,
And mirrors its own sweet splendor
  In numberless sparkling eyes.
But I see it fall more softly
  On a bowed, young, jetty head,
With a wondrous brow, and pensive eyes,
  And lips where the rose has fled:
And the maiden murmurs, in accents low,
In another tongue, a tale of woe.

Again I track its footsteps
  To a far Egyptian plain,
Where it falls in liquid glory
  Like a shower of silver rain.
And it haloes the grand, old Pyramids,
  In their mighty, solemn state,
And it calls up, within my spirit,
  The dead, and the ancient great.

And yonder, in far Arabia,
  It silvers the wondrous palm,
And rests on Sahara's sand waves
  With a heavy, baptismal calm.

Then back o'er the foaming ocean,
　As the billows dance in light,
I see it bathe the steamer,
　In her onward, steady flight ;
And it looks in the cabin window
　And wakes up the sailor boy,
Who has wandered away, and, homesick,
　Was dreaming of future joy.

Down the Rocky Mountain passes
　It shines with a cheering ray,
And, tangled amid the forest,
　It waits for the coming day ;
And so through the solemn minutes,
　While I rest from my spirit's flight,
Over the earth the Moonlight
　Is clasped in the arms of Night.

THE INEVITABLE.

By and by we shall be parted,
  By and by you'll go from me ;
You will go, my love, my darling,
  Leaving me but Memory.
Very blissful are the moments
  When you take me to your heart ;
Wretched, filled with dreary longing,
  When they bid us go apart.

O, my love, my life, my darling,
  How am I to live and do,
When the thorny road I travel
  Is not walked along with you?
How am I to bear the burden
  Of the heavy years and slow?
Who will interpose and save me
  From the cold world's cruel blow?

When the roses bloomed last summer,
  Where the river, rushing, ran,
Facing fearfully the future,
  Then this love for you began.
And again I tell thee, darling,
  That this love will live for aye ;
Lips, nor eyes, nor white hands' clasping,
  E'er will lead my heart astray.

Every thought, emotion, passion,
  Lives in me but by your word ;
Life, to me, has deeper meaning
  Since your breath its currents stirred.
But, alas ! you'll leave me, darling,
  Not *forget*, that *cannot* be !
For though interest bind you elsewhere,
  Still your *heart* must cling to me.

THE ROSY WINE CUP.

O, TOUCH not the rosy wine cup,
    Though its brilliance should charm thine eye,
For he who shall drink its contents
    Has opened a way to die.
Not die as the *world* might call it,
    But die to the good and true,
And blunt all the fine perceptions
    That ever ennobled you.

There is power in the rosy wine cup
    To send through the heart and brain
Bewildering thrills of pleasure,
    Dispelling the bosom's pain.
But 'twill only return more sharply
    When the fire of the wine has passed,
For the dreams that it may awaken
    Are only too bright to last.

O, trust not your power of keeping
    Yourself from the shoals before!
Your strength, in an evil moment,
    May leave you forevermore;
For the wine cup has conquered millions,
    And the loftiest minds of earth
Have sunk to the lowest level
    From a glass in an hour of mirth.

There are desolate homes where the demon
  Of drink has destroyed their light,
There are hearts that have loved too fondly,
  And bowed 'neath the wine cup's blight;
Put aside, then, the sparkling poison,
  For though danger seems far away,
You will bless, in some happy future,
  The dawn of your Temperance day.

13

TO DICK.

BECAUSE I hold your lightest word
  Of greater value far than gold,
Because I love you, would I hear,
  Each day, the story never old.
We never tire of sunset skies
  Which crimson with a radiance rare,
We never weary of sweet sounds,
  And sights of earth, divinely fair.

And fairer than the lily's snows,
  More lovely than the diamond's light,
Are words made eloquent with love,
  And looks which gild the darkest night.
The human heart, for aye, will yearn
  For that which love will yearn to give ;
Then chide me not because I crave
  Affection's words each day I live.

SONG OF THE WANDERER.

I SING on the mountains, I chant by the sea;
There are beauty and love for all beings but me;
I scale the white peaks that are covered with snow,
I traverse the valleys that nestle below;
I sail down the lengths of the rivers that wind
Like bands of blue ribbon, but naught do I find
Of beauty that *cheers* me, or love that's my own,
As I wander disheartened from zone unto zone.

I gaze on the glaciers, so massive and bright,
As they roll on their course in their wondrous might;
I watch for the gleam of the earliest star
Which gems the bright hills of an island afar,
Where the breezes are fragrant with ordorous balm,
And the ocean has sunk to the sleepiest calm;
But naught do I find that will answer to me,
Save the wild, weary moan of the slumbering sea.

I wander through halls where the rich and the proud
Make merry the days with a merriment loud;
I tread my way slowly along the full street
And stare at the faces and forms that I meet;
I dance off the hours 'mid a gay laughing crowd,
Or bend with a tear over many a shroud,
But nothing of pity or love is my own,
For I am forever and ever alone.

'Tis little to me though the sky may be blue,
Since I cannot believe that one being is true ;
The flowers may be painted in colors most rare,
I look at them sadly, for what do *I* care?
And music may yield most voluptuous sound,
While earth with a garland of beauty is crowned ;
I know not, I care not for sound or for sight,
Since I wander alone from the morn till the night.

THE PAST.

THE Past, O the Past! it wakes in the soul
A thousand strong feelings beyond our control;
It thrills through the breast like a magical spell,
And brings up the friends we have loved but too well.

A moonbeam may stray o'er the path which we tread,
And bring up the face and the form of our dead;
The fragrance of roses may bring back the tone
Of a beautiful song when the singer is gone.

How oft, like a shock, slight things bring to mind
The hours and the days we have left far behind;
Bright hours that were steeped in a halo of bliss,
Whose remembrance but deepens the darkness of
    this.

O, the beautiful Past! when the present shall be
Engulfed in the billows of Time's restless sea,
With the same fond regret we shall dream and de-
    plore
That the dear vanished hours will return nevermore.

When my years shall be more, and my love shall
    be less,
When I call to mind calmly lost kiss and caress,
Yet still in my heart, while its life pulses beat,
Shall some hours of the past be redeemingly sweet.

OCTOBER.

October sat on her gorgeous throne,
  With her lustrous eyes and her yellow hair,
And heard, with a glad and glowing smile,
  Each sound that rose on the pulsing air.
The gracious folds of her royal robe
  Were gemmed with pearls of the sparkling light;
Her cheeks were red with a blush of flame,
  And warm winds danced on her bosom white.

The sun went down, and his splendor fell
  In long bright waves o'er the year's sweet bride;
Then eyelids drooped, and the soft hands grasped
  A harp which the month of March had tried.
'Twas then that October sang a song
  Which sank down deep in the hearts of men,
For lovers fled to their trysting trees,
  And poets took up the waiting pen.

I am crowned with the wealth of the summer hours,
  I am drunken with draughts of the rosy wine;
I have breathed the breath of the fragrant flowers,
  And the best of the world it has all been mine.
I have eaten and drank through the long bright
    hours,
  I have eaten the fruit, I have drank the wine;

But I feel chill winds in the perfumed bowers,
  And I know that the chill has a sound and sign.

I have dallied with love that is fresh and free,
  I have pillowed my head on the Summer's breast;
The earth, and the sky, and the winds, and the sea,
  Have sung to me songs as I sank to rest.
From morn till night, from the night till the morn,
  I have lived out a life-time of wild excess;
Though the month which will come from the storms
      is born,
  Yet the poets and lovers will love it less.

I shall die, I shall die as a Queen of old;
  Death comes in a sleepy and sensuous form;
I am crowned, I am clad with the yellow gold,
  And the world's applause cometh up like a storm.
Sleep has flown — Death comes, but it brings to me
      bliss,
  For poets, and painters, and lovers will mourn,
As I breathe out my life in a long, sweet kiss,
  And afar through Eternity's gates am borne.

THE VOLUNTEER'S WIFE TO HER HUSBAND.

HENRY, dearest, roaming over
 Soil so far from wife and home,
Battling for our banner's glory,
 And the ages yet to come, —
Do not think I e'er forget thee,
 That my bosom's love grows cold;
For within its holiest recess
 Lives for thee a love untold.

You, afar, perchance are dreaming
 Sadly of your wife and child,
While your ear drinks in the thunder
 Of the battle fierce and wild.
But however fondly dreaming,
 Dream you ne'er more fond than I;
My devotion for you, dearest,
 Is a feeling ne'er will die.

O, my husband, should you ever
 Stand amid the battle's strife,
Know my lips are ever breathing
 Prayers for your too precious life.
God protect you in the battle,
 As beneath our Flag you fight,
And return you home in safety
 To my arms some summer night.

BY THE SEA.

ALONE by the sounding sea I sit,
  And my love he has gone afar from me ;
So rage ye winds, and war ye waves,
  In your own grand majesty.
I saw his barque, with the sails all set,
  Steer proudly past the harbor's bar ;
I waved him adieu, but my eyes were wet,
  For he followed the light of a false, false star.

The fishermen come and they look at me,
  As I sit on a rock and shade my eyes ;
For somehow they know — and they pity me —
  That my love was false as the summer skies.
How grandly the great waves rise and foam
  O'er the track which his ship left long ago ! —
E'en the fisherman sighs as he seeks his home
  And leaves me with face like the winter's snow.

They say the ocean has treacherous deeps,
  That sirens sit on the rocks and sing ;
Yet this is not why I shall wait and weep
  For a love which the tide will never bring.
There are tropic lands when the sea is passed,
  And a thousand nameless things to dread,
But what are any or all of these
  To her who mourns for a love long dead !

TO A LADY.

FROM HER LOVER.

O LADY, of the pure, pale face,
  And eyes of liquid light,
I am quite sure I lost, for you,
  My heart, on New Year's night ;
For from your face outshone a soul
  That elevated mine ;
How could I then refuse to bow
  Before so pure a shrine ?

I have, e'en now, within my heart,
  A picture of thy smile ;
Methought that none was e'er so sweet,
  Or quite so free from guile.
A hovering halo seemed to wreathe
  Around your regal head : —
Your lips seemed whispering of heaven,
  Though not a word you said.

Yes, lady, 'mong the gathered crowd,
  Your face seemed purest, best ;
I'm sure if one could win your love,
  That love would bring sweet rest.
But no ! the thought of earthly love
  Is not for such as thou,

Else would not such angelic grace
  Beam o'er that spotless brow.

Then pardon, lady, pardon this
  Perhaps unworthy rhyme :
Yet know one heart will treasure thee
  Throughout the years of time ;
And should we ever meet again,
  As on that New Year's night,
Pray bend on me, with kinder glance,
  Those eyes of liquid light.

FRIGHTENED.

TELL me, tell me, man of science,
  Am I blind forever, say?
Shall I no more see the faces
  I have loved for many a day?
Are the fields, so green and pleasant,
  Shut from me for evermore?
Shall I no more see the river
  And its dark-green bending shore?

Has God shut the blue sky from me,
  With its panoply of stars?
And destroyed my sight forever,
  And disfigured me with scars?
I who worship beauty madly
  In the heavens, the earth, the sea,
Tell me truly, without feigning,
  Is it ever shut from me?

Morning's beauty, evening's glory,
  Shall I nevermore behold?
Never gaze with olden rapture
  On their purple, blue, and gold?
I shall smell the sweet, sweet roses,
  But will they be shut from sight?

Can I be content in living
    When the day has turned to night?

Blind! O, word of wretched meaning!
    Do the blind not suffocate?
My bewildered brain will scarcely
    Comprehend this awful fate.
Will your love outlive this judgment?
    I shall need it so much more
When I'm blind to what the future
    Darkly holds for me in store.

I remember every footpath,
    Every blossom, every tree,
Where, in days of light and loving,
    I have strayed alone with thee.
Then you praised my eyes' rare beauty,
    When I bent them upon you;
Darling, will you now be tender,
    Just as kind to me, and true?

Ah! I'm weeping as I'm thinking
    All my pleading may be vain;
Did the doctor tell you, truly,
    That I should not see again?·
"No," you say?   O, word of gladness!
    I shall see your face once more; •
I've not lost your love, my darling —
    We'll be happy as of yore.

Yet, beloved one, I've been thinking,
    Lying lonely, shut from sight,

That I'd sooner give my eyesight
  Than the love you pledged one night.
I could bear the darkness calmly,
  Meek and patient as a child ;
'Twas the thought that I might lose you
  Which has made me nearly wild.

THE WANDERER'S CHRISTMAS.

'Tis Christmas night in cot and hall,
  'Tis Christmas night at sea,
'Tis Christmas night, o'er all the earth,
  For every one but me.
I see the village lights that gleam
  From many happy homes,
I know that there are smiles of love,
  For all save one who roams.

'Tis Christmas night among the rich,
  'Tis Christmas with the poor,
For all have some to love and greet
  Save I who walk the moor.
I know the Christmas trees are hung
  With presents, fair to see,
Bestowed by loving hearts and hands
  On every one but me.

Wide open swing the castle gates,
  And troops of guests go in,
But I am shut from happiness
  As if it were a sin.
Gay groups of lovers come and go
  Beneath the starlit sky,
But I, — I wander to and fro,
  And wander but to die.

I sit upon the marble steps
  Of stately homes of wealth,
· And when the door swings wide
  I look on merry youth and health.
The skies flame out with northern lights,
  But bitter is the cold ;
O, would that I might walk, to-night,
  The city paved with gold.

My tattered clothes, amid the blast,
  Blow wildly here and there,
And though my lips are stiff and blue,
  I strive to frame a prayer.
This is the night when Christ came down
  To save a world of woe ;
But ah ! it brings no joy to me
  Amid this blinding snow.

I've toiled so long without repay
  That I am weak and faint ;
And yet, to any ear on earth,
  I dare not make complaint.
O, rich men, sitting in your halls,
  O, women, proud and fair,
Pray God that you may never know
  What I am called to bear !

Your lights send · out upon the snow
  A bright and cheery ray,
Which is but mockery to one
  Who has nowhere to stay.

I trusted night would cool the pulse
  That beats so hot and high ;
It will ; I hear it whispered low
  That I am soon to die.

I wonder if 'tis Christmas night
  Above, beyond the blue ;
And are there any presents there
  For me, as well as you ?
Ah, me, my pulse is beating slow,
  I can no longer roam ;
O Christ! this Christmas night take Thou
  The weary wanderer home.

Ah, list ! I hear the angels sing,
  I see their harps of gold,
All pain is gone, no longer I
  Can feel the bitter cold.
The gates swing wide, I see a face
  Bend to me, dazzling bright :
Praise God! the wanderer will be
  In heaven this Christmas night.

14

THE WHEEL OF LIFE.

BEHOLD the world goes on and on,
  Behold the world goes over!
There are some who live in thistles,
  And some who live in clover,
And one who was at first a friend
  May prove at last a lover.

How strangely doth the world move on,
  With mingled joy and sorrow!
Some hearts there are beat hopefully
  And wait a glad to-morrow,
And there are some who never hope,
  But always trouble borrow.

'Tis e'er the same with high and low,
  With prince and toiling peasant;
One class has much, and one has naught,
  And neither find all pleasant,
But most are looking on and on
  Beyond the fleeting present.

So moves the world in sun and shade,
  With change at every station;
The artist-poet paints alone,
  The world lives his creation, —
But artist, subject, all, alike
  Must serve their own probation.

Adieu, good friends ; when all is done,
  And we our work have ended,
However hopeful we have been
  That grace and good were blended,
Some clearer light will show to us
  Much we could wish amended.